A
Harlequin
Romance

CITADEL
OF SWALLOWS

by

GWEN WESTWOOD

HARLEQUIN BOOKS   TORONTO
WINNIPEG

Original hard cover edition published in 1973
by Mills & Boon Limited

© Gwen Westwood 1973

SBN 373-01716-2

Harlequin edition published September 1973

Printed in Canada

CHAPTER ONE

Two young women, each very attractive in a totally different way, leaned against the rail of the cruise ship as the beat of its engines slowed its tempo. From the deck they could see the island with its broken columns glittering silver against the deep blue of the sky, and around them the Aegean Sea had the luminous sheen of a purple grape.

'Ruins again!' moaned Lauren. 'What's so wonderful about the place anyway? It looks like a marble quarry!'

Her dark red hair with its elaborate coils and waves was hardly dishevelled by the breeze that brought with it the scent of thyme. In her cream corded slacks suit with its silk scarf in the shade of emerald that matched her eyes, she looked more suited to stroll along some crowded fashionable street, the Via Veneto or the Champs Elysées, rather than be preparing for a visit to an uninhabited island that was only three miles across. Only her huge sunglasses were a concession to the occasion and to the brilliant light that poured down from the cloudless sky.

'Delos,' Stacey said rather dreamily. For once she was not going to be put off by Lauren's cool contempt for anything that did not amuse her. 'Our first Greek island.'

Her eyes glowed deep brown with as luminous a radiance as the air around her. Honey-gold tendrils of hair escaped from their knot and blew across her forehead.

'I was a fool to book us on this four-day tour,' grumbled Lauren. 'I didn't realize we would be faced with so much walking.'

'But I rather enjoy sightseeing,' said Stacey.

'It's not for me. But the ordinary ferry boats are so primitive. I understood this would be a luxury ship. What a laugh! If I'd known I would have to queue for meals with loud-voiced trippers I would have chosen a more direct route. It simply hasn't been worth it.'

Stacey did not answer. She could not decide whether she was glad or sorry that the arrival at Colin's island was to be delayed for a few days by their visits to other places on this Aegean cruise. She longed to see him and yet felt scared too. Would she feel the same to him or he to her? Six months ago she would have laughed if anyone had told her she would be unsure. Of course she had been thrilled when Colin's sister, Lauren, had suggested she should accompany her on this assignment to model clothes in Athens and to follow this by visiting the island where Colin was writing his best-seller.

Surely when they met everything would be marvellous. Letters were always so unsatisfactory and she understood quite well that he had not been able to write very much, because, as he had explained, when your trade is writing and you are busy with this all day, it is difficult to write letters in your spare time.

'Are you going ashore?' Stacey asked hopefully and yet hesitantly. She knew Lauren was not keen on this kind of sightseeing and preferred something more gay.

'I suppose we may as well. I don't seem to be able to get up a four for bridge. It's the first island we've touched at, and you know what these Americans are like about seeing ruins. They think anything over a hundred years old is a miracle of beauty.'

'This existed in about 500 B.C. That's a little more than a hundred years ago,' Stacey protested. She was glad she was going to be allowed to see the island and not going to be dragged into another game of bridge.

'I hope you remembered to complain about the bathroom once more,' said Lauren. 'It doesn't seem to have had much effect up to now.'

'Yes. I told them that every time we use the shower the bathroom floods. But I don't know whether the purser understood me. He smiled very charmingly and said he would do something.'

'Really, Stacey, you should try to be a bit more emphatic and not be led astray by all this Greek charm. They're all too handsome, that's the trouble. But they have no idea of efficiency.'

The pretty white cruise ship had anchored some way from the old harbour and small motorboats had come out to meet the passengers who were crowding the deck, their chatter in a variety of languages sounding like the harsh noise of the seagulls that were flying around surveying the scene.

For different reasons, Stacey because she was shy and Lauren because she held aloof from the rabble, as she called the majority of her fellow passengers, they were on the last boatload to leave the ship. And when they landed on the island they found that their guide had set out already, leaving a message that they must hasten to catch up with the rest.

'I refuse to follow that mob,' declared Lauren. 'We'll just wander around on our own. I don't care two hoots about the island's history, anyway, but I thought it would be a good idea for us to stretch our legs on dry land. Let's sit for a while until they're out of sight, otherwise we'll have some busybody coming back for us.'

They sat on one of the numerous marble blocks and Stacey raised her face to the sun. She felt very far from London and the world of fashion as she breathed in the pure crystal air. The desolate island with its littered ruins had a startling white radiance in the afternoon light, and all around them, pushing up past the broken colonnades, wild barley grass and vivid red poppies grew. Stacey looked at Lauren hoping that she was not intending to sit here all afternoon. She herself was anxious to explore this strange place and it was clear from the haste of the guide that there was not much time scheduled for this halt in the voyage.

But Lauren was gazing at a group of men sitting near the jetty engaged in some task connected with their fishing nets.

'Just look at those gorgeous men,' she said. 'Even the Greek workmen look like gods sometimes.'

She spoke in a loud voice and Stacey found herself blushing.

'Hush, Lauren! They'll hear you.'

Lauren laughed.

'If they did it's hardly likely they understand English. No one lives on this island permanently. They must be fishermen from Mykonos – it's only five miles away. We're going to anchor off there this evening.'

Stacey gave a quick glance at the group of four or five men, olive-skinned, with clear-cut features and dark curly hair showing from under their peaked caps. They wore dark denim type trousers and sweaters and certainly their outdoor type of rugged good looks, their vivacity and animation as they talked to each other, was very attractive. One man was mending a net, with one leg stretched out, brown toes curled in the meshes, lifting and holding up the part upon which he was working. The others seemed to be having a meal consisting of coarse bread, white cheese and olives, every now and again pausing to take a good swallow from a flagon of wine.

They were not slow in appreciating the fact that there were two pretty women in their vicinity. There were glances in their direction and some comments.

'Do come, Lauren,' urged Stacey, made brave by her confusion. 'Surely we've sat here long enough. We'll never have time to see everything if we don't move soon.'

Lauren rose to go. The path led past the group of fishermen and as they came level with them there was a murmur of greeting to which they could hardly not respond with a smile. Stacey noticed that there was only one man who failed to look at them. He was a taller man than the rest, with aquiline features, a straight nose and the half smiling mouth that is seen on old Greek statues which can almost be interpreted as a sneer.

When they had passed, the conversation of the men seemed to increase but was suddenly quelled by some comment from this older man. Lauren was used to the homage of men. She was used to admiration and was piqued if she did not see it in the eyes of even the most humble of them. She was like a queen, thought Stacey, holding court, very sure of her own beauty and charm. But she herself had hardly escaped yet from the tongue-tied embarrassment she had suffered at school on account of her shyness. Work at the dress designer's establishment had only increased her feeling of inferiority, for her job was of the humblest. If you wished to get on in a concern such as this you had to start at the lowest rung, Lauren had assured her. She was a kind of Girl Friday, who did all the work that no one else wanted to do, even to picking up pins and making tea. It was only because Lauren was a very favoured model that they had been persuaded to release her to accompany her on this journey.

Now Stacey was conscious of the eyes of the fishermen, although they seemed courteous enough. She wished she could be a little less self-conscious about meeting people. It was so difficult on board ship. Lauren sent her on errands and she found it hard even to get up courage to speak to the officials about Lauren's numerous complaints, let alone be firm with them.

They had come to a place on the island that seemed a great square of littered ruins and her attention was diverted from thoughts of herself.

'Oh, look,' she said. 'Those must be the marble lions. I read about them in a book in the ship's library.'

'Lions?' said Lauren. 'They look more like greyhounds.'

'No, not greyhounds. Panthers,' suggested Stacey.

There were five of them. Shining white beasts with long lean flanks, crouching to spring in the way they had been carved over two thousand years ago when they had been placed there to guard the sacred way that the pilgrims took to the shrine of the god. The caverns of their mouths that were open to roar seemed a dark contrast to the rest of their bodies, which were made of brilliant Naxian marble streamlined by the winds of centuries.

'Could we go to the top of the hill?' asked Stacey. 'We'll be able to see the whole island from there. It's not awfully steep.'

'It may not be, but I think I'll stay here. Oh, look, there's Elspeth van Dyk.'

Sitting on one of the pieces of marble was the woman with whom they had played bridge last night. She greeted them with enthusiasm.

'I've sure seen enough of ruins for one day,' she told them, fanning her cheeks with her hat of woven straw. 'I'm going back to wait for the first launch to the ship. Otherwise I declare I'm going to land back in Georgia with a heart condition.'

'I'll come with you,' said Lauren, who already seemed to have tired of the expedition. 'What about you, Stacey?'

'I'd like to see more of the island. Do you mind if I stay a little longer?'

'You go along, dear,' said the American lady before Lauren had time to object. 'Your legs are younger than mine. There's not much to see, though. But the mosaic pictures on the floors of the houses are impressive. It seems they decorated them that way instead of using rugs. Seems a chilly idea. I must say I'd rather have wall-to-wall carpeting any day!'

Most of the passengers seemed to be wending their way back to the ship when Stacey proceeded to explore the rest of the island. Now she was alone she could appreciate the strange wonder of Delos. The broken columns with wild grass, poppies and yellow thistles growing through them seemed iridescent with shining radiance. And soon she came to the remains of houses with their wonderful mosaics. The colours seemed as vivid as if they had been created a few days ago — a ferocious panther snarling, a dolphin twining himself around a sea-god's trident.

It was an easy climb up to the top of Mount Cynthos, the small hill barely four hundred feet higher than its surroundings but seeming on this island that was so small to be much higher than it actually was.

As Stacey walked by gentle steps along the pathway, she trod upon sage and thyme, and the scent of these and other strong-scented herbs was all around her. Large blackish lizards watched her approach, then darted into their crevices. Near the top of the rise, she sat down and took time to observe the scene. From here she could look down on the whole of the ruined area, the pillars, the broken walls, all that remained of the once proud and sacred city.

The sun was going down over the island of Syros in the west. Upon the horizon were other islands, violet in the evening light, the group of the Cyclades of which small Delos is the centre. Stacey could see some people in the distance, but to her they seemed unimportant compared to the vast stretch of the ghostly city. She had read a little about the island and she knew how on the anniversary of Apollo's birth in May, the great festival took place here. A convoy of ships came to the island from Athens, with priests, sacred choirs and dancing girls. They would go in procession to the temple of Apollo. She imagined the town thronged with people, tall soldiers, charioteers, flute girls, slaves and pilgrims. And in those days the temple would have been bright with colours, rich in carving and gold.

Her thoughts came back to the present day, or rather the immediate past. Was it wise, she thought for the hundredth time in the last few days, to go to see Colin? When she had first come to London she had stayed with Lauren on the strength of an old friendship between their two mothers and she had met Colin for the first time. She had never before met a man with such sophistication, such easy charm, and she was flattered by his attentions, especially since she knew that many girls were interested in him.

One thing that worried her a little was that he did not seem to remain in any particular job for very long, but when he had declared his intention of going to a Greek island for a few months to write a book, she was pleased in spite of the fact that they would have to part for a while. She was sure he could write a best-seller as he had assured her he would. She did not believe it when Lauren, who knew little of her interest in Colin, told her he was leaving England for the next few months because the parents of one of his girl-friends were getting a little too pressing about marriage. Had he not said himself that she was the only girl with whom he could contemplate spending a lifetime?

Of course she had not told Lauren anything of Colin's attentions. He had made her promise to keep it secret until they could announce their engagement. She fully appreciated his reasons and had even prevailed upon him to accept some of her savings, assuring him that he could pay her back when his book was published. It had been hard after that to scrape up enough money to come here, but she had managed it, and Lauren had been kind about expenses, although she had expected a full return in services of one kind and another.

A cool wind was rising, bending the wild grasses and flecking the deep blue sea with white foam. Stacey realized that she was alone. The other people from the boat had disappeared towards the jetty and the colour of the sky was deepening to violet whereas a few moments ago it seemed the whole hillside had been afire with the setting sun.

She rose to go, and clearly in the cool air came the voices of bullfrogs croaking with a booming sound that was almost menacing. The lizards had disappeared with the sunlight. She knew she should go and yet she was reluctant to tear herself away. Her attention was caught by a cave nearby. This must be the Sacred Cavern, an old rock temple, possibly the first one to be used on the island for the worship of the gods. She had read of this in the book, but surely this dark place had been used for another purpose, not for the cult of Apollo, the god of radiant light? It was dark and gloomy and Stacey could imagine frightening rites, even blood sacrifices, taking place within the rough granite walls.

Just as she was thinking this, she heard the bleat of a young kid. It seemed so much in accordance with what she had been thinking that for a moment she thought she had imagined it. But no, there it was again coming from inside the cavern. It sounded distressed and she could not bring herself to leave it. Suppose it was stuck in a crevice? From the setting sun there was a ray of light penetrating the gloomy cave and she could just see a small white animal struggling to get out. She went inside, and as quickly the sun disappeared and she felt again the oppressive atmosphere of a place long dead to human occupation.

Suddenly the pictures of the island that Stacey had conjured up seemed too vivid, the inhabitants who had been dead a thousand years seemed too real. She longed to be back upon the ship with Lauren telling her sharply to stop dreaming. She picked up the little goat and, as it struggled frantically, kicking out at her, she turned hastily to get out of the cave. The sky beyond the entrance was the deep colour of a ripe aubergine and all at once there was a darker shadow, a figure that filled the narrow aperture with its tall menacing shape.

She uttered an involuntary shriek of terror and there was a startled exclamation. It was no ghost, then, but still she trembled with fright as she recognized that the tall figure in the dark clothes was one of the fishermen, the tall one of the group, and she felt very isolated as he advanced towards her across the dark cave.

But he spoke in English.

'So, you have found Flavia. That is good.'

'Is that her name? She seems very tame.'

For the little goat was nestling against her now, seeming quite contented.

'She is a child's pet. How do you say in English . . . very spoiled. But you . . . what are you doing here alone?'

'I . . . I was curious to see the Sacred Cave. But now I must be going. I have to get back to the ship.'

'And how will you do that?'

Close to her in the half light his face looked even more like one of those Greek statues with its lips curling in such a fashion that you could not decide whether it smiled or sneered.

'Why . . . why, I'll walk back to the launch. Why do you ask?'

'Because the launches left some time ago. And the ship itself is just weighing anchor. Look.'

Stacey started violently as he touched her shoulder,

turning her around and guiding her to the opening of the cave. In the gathering dusk the small white steamer in the bay was moving, gradually gathering speed. It looked like a toy, certainly too far away to be hailed and forced to stop.

A feeling of blind panic descended upon Stacey. What on earth was she to do? How incredibly stupid she had been to wander all this way. And now she was left alone on an island where no one lived and there was no person in sight except this tall fisherman who looked like a Corsican pirate even if he did speak English. She could not imagine he would be sorry for her plight. But he was the only person who could help her. 'What can I do?' she asked. 'I must get back to the ship. My cousin will be missing me.'

But would she? If Stacey had started a bridge session it was quite likely that she would not be missed until dinner, which was taken after nine o'clock.

'Your cousin is the one who admires Greek men. And you?'

Stacey remembered with shame Lauren's comments about the group of fishermen. She looked at her companion's face and was unable to interpret the sneering smile. Who was he? He was dressed in fishermen's clothes and yet his English was too good for an uneducated man, unless of course he had travelled, as most Greeks seemed to do. Maybe he had been in America, though his accent seemed to deny that.

'I don't know any Greek men,' she said in confusion.

'We must remedy that. And now how would you like to cross to Mykonos? My brother and I are taking our boat over and your ship will anchor off the island this evening.'

Her relief, after the frightening few moments she had just experienced, was tremendous.

'Would you really take me? Oh, how good of you!'

The smile remained, enigmatic, elusive.

'Did you think we would leave you on the island? You have a strange idea of Grecian manners. But, as you say, you do not know us. Now come. We must go or it will be quite dark before we get to Mykonos.'

They made their way down towards the old jetty. The man had taken the burden of the little goat from her, but he made no attempt to reconcile his long stride to her shorter one and she had some difficulty in keeping up with him. She wondered whether he expected her to walk behind him as she had seen the peasant women following their men on the Greek mainland. But when she had trailed behind for some distance he stopped impatiently to hurry her on.

At the jetty only one man remained, and although he was shorter there was a distinct family resemblance, the same classical dark features, but the expression was not as forbidding. Indeed it was distinctly charming, when he smiled.

'So you found her,' he exclaimed, looking at the kid. 'And someone else too.'

His glance was admiring and appraising. The older man frowned at him and spoke sharply in Greek. But the younger man seemed not in the least disconcerted and went to help Stacey into a small dinghy which was quickly pushed off and rowed towards a smartly painted caïque with furled reddish brown sails. The small kid was tethered to the side, bleating plaintively. The sails were hoisted and off they skimmed into the brisk wind.

The older man took no further notice of Stacey, but as soon as they had settled the boat to an even course the younger one turned and regarded her with undisguised interest. He began to question her.

'What is your name?'

'Stacey Grant.'

He tried to pronounce it, hesitating a little over the unfamiliar words.

'It is pretty. It suits you. And you are English, yes?'

'Yes,' she assented.

'Are you married?'

'No.'

'You have boy-friend?'

'I . . . no.' She was confused and would not confide her interest in Colin to a total stranger.

'So . . . I thought all pretty girls had boy-friends in England. It is – how they say – a permissive society. Not as in Greece. In Greece it is very important that a girl remains chaste until married.'

She flushed and felt a little indignant. But how could she explain anything of her life to him?

'And do you live with your family?'

'No. I live in London where I work.'

The other man interrupted them, speaking sharply to his brother and then turning to her.

'My brother must concentrate on the sailing now. I should be glad if you would not talk any more.'

Well, really! Who was it who was doing the cross-examination? thought Stacey. She gladly turned away and looked ahead at the shape of the island dark against the purple sky. The sails were furled and they started to approach under motor. No wonder that the bigger ships had to stay outside the harbour. It was like being on a bucking horse as the boat mounted each wave and slapped down on the other side.

And then they were in calmer waters and the circular stretch of the quay was visible with the lights already beginning to twinkle and show up the white buildings on the edge of the sea.

'Your ship will take longer to get here, because it had to go out into deeper water, but you can expect your friends to be here quite soon,' the older man said.

Stacey was seized with panic again, but this time the cause was simply material. She supposed she would have to offer to pay the two men for her unexpected sail and she knew she only had a handful of drachmas in her purse, for Lauren was the one who took charge of the money, merely handing it out when it was necessary for Stacey to settle their accounts. She would have to promise to pay them later, arrange to meet them in the evening. But that would be embarrassing.

'So . . .' the younger man was saying as they stood on the quayside. 'How you like Mykonos?'

'It looks like something from a film set,' said Stacey. 'But lovely,' she hastened to add in case her words had sounded patronizing.

'It is better in the daytime. Then the white houses dazzle your eyes in the sunlight.'

She looked at him, a little surprised at his eloquence, but all Greeks seemed to be surprising people. In the dim light the quayside showed a sweeping curve of whitewashed buildings with shops still open displaying vivid handwoven goods and heavy knitted sweaters in natural cream-coloured wool. The evening was mild and people were sitting at tables in the street, eating and drinking. Stacey was all at once aware that she would love to sit down too. She was tired and hungry after the afternoon's trials. But first she must thank her rescuers. Already the older man was looking restless, seeming anxious to get away.

'I must thank you very much indeed,' she spoke hesitantly. 'Of course I must pay you for your trouble, but unfortunately I have very little money with me. Perhaps I could arrange to leave it at one of the shops or . . .'

The older man gave an exclamation of annoyance. Oh dear, did he think she was trying to get out of paying for the trip? But the younger one made a sound that was like 'po-po-po-po' and laughed.

'You do not have to pay us. We had to come here in any case. But you can reward me by having dinner with me this evening, yes?'

What could she do? It would be most ungrateful to say no to him. And there could surely be no harm in it, though Lauren would hardly be pleased when she came ashore to find Stacey dining with a Greek fisherman.

He spoke a few words in Greek to his brother, who still seemed disapproving, and then he turned to Stacey.

'I will take you to a good friend of mine where you can – how do the English say it – "wash and brush up", and I will come for you in a little while when I have fixed the boat. By the way, I am Niko and my brother is Stavros.'

The 'good friend' was the wife of the owner of one of the *tavernas*, the eating houses by the quayside, and Stacey was welcomed with almost as much enthusiasm as her companion. Stavros had remained with the boat and Niko excused himself from accepting a glass of wine, saying he would be back very soon.

Stacey tidied up as best she could and combed her hair in front of a small mirror in a bedroom furnished with a large bed covered by a handwoven quilt of many colours, while she was being watched by a group of curious dark-eyed children. When she came back to sit at a table outside the *taverna* she could see that the ship had anchored outside the bay. She knew that the passengers were to have dinner first before embarking for an evening on Mykonos, and she was worried about Lauren's reaction when she realized she was missing. But there was little she could do.

'Hallo there.' Niko stood before her. He had changed from his fishing clothes into dark slacks and a scarlet sweater and with his curly black hair and smiling handsome face he looked a very presentable escort, she thought. Even Lauren could hardly object.

'My brother managed to radio your ship and they know you are safe,' he went on.

'That was very kind of him. I was worrying about my friends' feelings. I had no idea you would be able to send a radio message.'

'Oh, yes, you see we are not so primitive as you think.'

He was smiling in a teasing way. He really was very handsome, she thought. But dangerously flirtatious even to her inexperienced view. The way he looked at her, the expression of his eyes, the manner in which he caressed her elbow as he led her to a more preferable table, all set up warning red lights signalling in her brain. But she reassured herself that she need never see him again after tonight and soon her travelling companions would be here and she could take her leave of him.

For a fisherman he seemed to be very sophisticated, but then she had no acquaintance with Greek men at all so she was not able to judge him.

'What will you drink?' he asked. 'You like Greek wines?'

'I haven't tried them yet,' she confessed. 'But please, nothing too strong.'

He smiled. 'Then we will not give you ouzo. Perhaps you would like to try a little retsina?'

Before she could say yes or no, the waiter had brought a flagon to the table and she was being pressed to sip the golden wine that was impregnated with the distinct resinous flavour.

'It's like drinking a pine forest,' she laughed surprised, and he was obviously pleased.

'Most foreigners dislike it to begin with. It is, how you say, an acquired taste.'

The waiter arrived with a plate of small delicacies, minced meat wrapped in vine leaves, and small fingers of something fried in batter. He pressed her to try these and was delighted when she hungrily ate more.

'I'm glad you like one of our national dishes,' he commented.

'They're delicious. What are they?' she asked.

'Fried octopus. What else?' he replied.

For a few moments Stacey lost her hearty appetite. But soon the next course came, red mullet baked upon coals, and she found that equally tasty. The good food, the resinous wine, the general atmosphere of friendliness and good will, and the charm of the young man opposite her made her feel much more relaxed than usual. She forgot her shyness and found herself laughing and responding to his easy attraction. But a shadow fell across the table and a voice deeper than that of Niko said, 'So here you are.' She looked up into brown eyes, beautiful and dark as those of a Greek statue and just as cold. Niko looked displeased, but he called the waiter and Stavros ordered ouzo, the strong cloudy drink that had been rejected as unsuitable for Stacey.

'Your fellow passengers have already set out in the launches. You won't have long to wait now,' he said.

'He wants to get rid of me,' she thought. 'But he can hardly expect me to get up and leave until my meal is finished.'

'Thank you for sending the radio message,' she said gently.

'It was only sensible,' he replied.

With the arrival of Stavros, all her pleasure in Niko's company had gone. He really was a very disconcerting man, she thought, taking a secret glance at the brown face with its defined black brows below the curling dark hair.

There was a stir further down the quayside and she realized that the passengers had arrived off the ship. Now they came surging along the quay, spreading out like a flock of coloured butterflies as they examined the wares in the shops that were open to the street. And here was Lauren, poised and beautiful, in a white dress bordered in scarlet and a blazer to match slung carelessly over her shoulders. One would have thought it would clash with her hair, but it did not, only made it look more striking. Stacey excused herself from her companions and went towards her.

'Lauren, I'm here.'

'So I see. Well, I wouldn't have thought it of you,

23

Stacey. Imagine getting involved with those fishermen! I said they were handsome, but I didn't mean you to take it so seriously.'

Lauren succeeded in making Stacey feel embarrassed as usual. 'It wasn't like that at all,' she protested. 'They came to my rescue. If it hadn't been for them I don't know what I would have done. And, Lauren, I had to have dinner with one of them. I could hardly refuse when he'd been so kind. Please come over and meet them.'

She was afraid Lauren would say no, but of course she might have known she would appreciate being seen by her fellow passengers getting on with some of the local inhabitants. She came over to the table and the two men rose and looked at her. Stacey was used to the effect Lauren had on men. She was used to always finding herself in the background, but she could not help feeling a little disappointed like a child who wanted to say, 'I found them first.'

Soon they were all sitting and drinking more of the wine, though Stacey found it was better at this stage to accept a small cup of black bitter coffee served with a glass of iced water. A group of men started to play bouzouki music, plucking at the strings of the instruments that were shaped like mandolins and played with a plectrum. The clearcut brilliant tones re-echoed into the blue night between the walls of the whitewashed buildings and out towards the wine-dark sea.

The music was gay and yet had a haunting sadness. Suddenly Niko rose and quite alone in a small space of the crowded patio started to dance, his hands held up, fingers clasped, his feet pacing in slow time to the music. It should have looked ludicrous, the sight of one man solemnly dancing to himself, but it was strangely moving. First one, then another man joined him and they danced as they wanted to, creating their own steps to the plangent music of the bouzoukis. It was a far cry from the conventional dancing of the West and no woman, even amongst the visitors, ventured to join them.

Stacey glanced at Lauren. She was talking to Stavros, laughing and even succeeding in making him smile. When the dance was over she jumped up.

'We must go to buy something from those marvellous shops,' she said. 'Do come and help us.'

Stavros and Niko both smiled at her enthusiasm and seemed eager to obey her, and they strolled along the starlit front examining the cream-coloured knitted goods and the brilliant woven garments. Stavros and Lauren had gone on ahead and Stacey found herself alone with Niko. He took her arm in his caressing way.

'Why hurry? Are you so eager to buy these things from the shops?'

'Not really. In fact I have very little money with me.'

'I thought all you tourists were rich. But no matter. I am not interested in the shops either. Come, let me show you a typical street of Mykonos.'

He drew her along one of the narrow streets that led away from the quay. The houses were startlingly white, but the shadows were deep and dark. The street was paved with flat square stones so light that they, like the walls, seemed to glow in the night. Pots of geraniums and herbs stood beside the doors and beside them outside staircases led up on to the roofs. There seemed a magical quality about this night on a strange island. The bouzouki music thrilled with its plangent chords from the distant *taverna* and Stacey remembered how her companion had danced without selfconsciousness and with an outgoing joy in living.

She smiled at the thought and he who had been watching her stopped and slid his arm around her shoulders turning her gently towards him and lifting her face to look at it.

'Why did you smile?'

She tried to disengage herself, but found that she was firmly held.

'Oh, because I felt happy. Because I've never seen the Greek islands before and tonight has been a lovely experience. But I think we'd better go now. The others will be looking for us.'

'Not yet. Not quite yet.'

His mouth came down upon hers. There was nothing passionate about it, for Niko, experienced as he was with women, sensed her gentle innocence.

'Ah, that was good, was it not?'

She laughed, finding herself unable to be cross with him, for in a way he made her think of Colin.

'What a sweet thing you are, Stacey!'

He did not press her to stay but led the way back to the quay, his arm around her. There the passengers were waiting to re-embark and they could see Lauren and Stavros obviously looking for them. Niko dropped his arm from around Stacey's waist, but the older man had evidently noticed this, for he frowned and again spoke rather sharply to his younger brother. But already the people were pressing towards the launches and the pilots were calling 'All aboard!' and their farewells were of necessity hurried.

As they bumped over the curling dark waves towards the ship, Stacey could not regret that Niko had kissed her. It had been a charming interlude and she would never see him again. As for Stavros, she was sure she did not want to meet him ever again. She dismissed them both from her mind and thought of Colin. Soon she would be with him on another enchanted island and no one else would matter. He alone was the reason why she had come to Greece.

CHAPTER TWO

LAUREN stayed in bed next morning, only getting up in time for the pre-lunch aperitif. She had kept Stacey busy with various tasks and neither of them had been up on deck yet. Now she came storming out of the bathroom wearing a towel.

'The shower's awash again,' she complained. 'For heaven's sake, Stacey, why can't you impress on the purser that it simply doesn't work?'

'I'll go now,' Stacey promised. Because Lauren had used her influence to get Stacey included on this trip for which the firm had paid part of the expenses, she expected Stacey to render all the services she demanded.

Stacey was wearing a white pleated skirt and a purple ribbed top that revealed her tanned midriff and was scooped low at the neck. Lauren had handed it to her and she had thought it a little daring, but on the cruise ship it seemed natural to dress in a more casual fashion.

In the purser's office there was an open section where there was a counter and a screen partially concealing the inner sanctum. Stacey stood at the counter and waited for someone to take notice of her, but the men who were behind the screen were evidently having a pre-lunch drink with the purser, for there was a conversation in Greek going on, punctuated every now and again by deep laughter.

Stacey hesitated to interrupt, but decided she must be

strong-minded or she would never hear the last of it from Lauren. So she rapped smartly on the counter. There was an exclamation that did not sound very pleased and the purser's head appeared around the screen. But when he saw Stacey he advanced towards her with his usual charming smile.

'Miss Grant! How nice to see you. I can help you with something, perhaps?'

In his face there was no acknowledgment that she had made any previous request. Obviously she must start again.

'The shower ... the bath in our cabin ... it doesn't work ... it floods every time we use it.' Looking at the puzzled, uncomprehending expression on his face, she desperately resorted to a French idiom. 'The shower ... it does not work.'

He smiled. 'Why you not come to me before? Certainly two charming ladies cannot have any discomfort. I will see to it at once.'

She looked at him doubtfully. She had received this answer every time she had visited his office.

'Perhaps you could come and see for yourself.'

'Later, perhaps. Just now I am entertaining ...' he lowered his voice ... 'very distinguished guests, you understand ... how do you say it? V.I.P.s.'

Stacey reflected that it seemed rather odd to be entertaining distinguished guests in this small office, but one never knew. Just then a head came around the partition and to her utter surprise Niko said something in Greek that obviously meant 'Hurry. We're waiting to drink.' He did not see Stacey because she was hidden by the burly form of the purser. At the same time the lower voice of Stavros came from the other side making some remark. She was astonished and bewildered. What were they doing on the ship? They must have decided to come on to Rhodes. But why had the purser said solemnly that he had distinguished guests? He must have been joking. It took a lot to make her cross, but she felt annoyed now. First because Niko had said good-bye to her presumably knowing he was going to be on the ship. Then because the purser preferred to sit drinking with these fishermen friends rather than attend to his duties. She stood upright and said in a very determined manner, 'I've complained about this shower three times since we embarked on this ship. If you can't attend to it soon, we would like to be transferred to another cabin.'

The purser was all contrition. But he smiled regretfully and shook his head.

'I am very sorry, madam, but this is not possible. As you must have noticed, the ship is full to capacity and there is not another cabin to be had.'

She was startled to see the tall figure of Stavros looming behind the purser. His dark eyes showed no recognition and she could still not tell whether that half-smile held any cordiality. He asked the purser a question, obviously wanting an explanation of the scene. There was a discussion that sounded a little sharp, but it was all in Greek and Stacey reflected that in a foreign language often the talk sounds more emotional than it really is. Immediately after this he returned to his seat behind the partition.

'You are fortunate, madam,' the purser said. 'Mr. Demetrios has instructed me to give you and your companion the suite usually reserved for his family at no extra cost.'

'But . . . but I can't accept that . . . and anyway, who is Mr. Demetrios?'

The purser was obviously flabbergasted at her ignorance.

'Why, he is the owner of these ships, the whole shipping line. Madam has never heard of him?'

Of course she had heard of them. Who had not? Even in England their names made news, for they were Greek shipping magnates, not in the same class of wealth as Onassis or Niarchos, but wealthy and important enough.

'All I want,' she said, 'is some kind of cabin with a shower that works. I can't accept a luxury cabin.'

'But, madam,' the purser spread his arms wide, 'Kyrios Demetrios has ordered it and I cannot go against him. You will see you will have a beautiful cabin. You will much enjoy, yes?'

Stacey decided she would gain nothing by further argument. Lauren would probably be very pleased if they were put in a more pleasant cabin. She would think Stacey mad to refuse. But Stacey was in a very bewildered frame of mind. To think that she had thought Stavros and Niko were fishermen, and now it appeared they owned the shipping line!

After lunch a steward came to help move them. Lauren grumbled a little at the inconvenience of moving from one cabin to another, but even her complaints were stilled when she saw the accommodation they had been given.

'It must be their own private suite,' she said, and the steward confirmed this as they looked in admiration at the large cabin. The beds had bedheads of white quilted satin and there were damask coverlets and a pastel-

31

coloured carpet wreathed with roses. The bathroom had taps like silver dolphins and beautiful crystal fittings. Everything was of a much higher standard of luxury than they had had before.

'Kyrios Demetrios says he is sorry there are no flowers, but if he had known he would have ordered some from Athens.'

'What a pity,' said Lauren. 'That's all it needs.'

'Is Madam satisfied?' asked the steward. Stacey smiled. She was thinking of the shower that had plagued them for three days and the narrow cabin from which she had had to disappear whenever Lauren wished to dress.

'Quite satisfied,' she nodded, trying to look dignified. 'It will do very nicely.'

'I'll leave you to straighten things out,' said Lauren. She always made it quite clear that she expected Stacey to act as a lady's maid to her and she did not propose to unpack her own clothes.

It took Stacey some time to arrange their possessions and when she came up on deck the ship was approaching the island of Rhodes. The passengers were exclaiming at their first sight of the circular harbour with its ancient ramparts of golden stone.

Lauren was standing at the bow of the ship with Niko by her side. He looked distinctly different from the dark-clad fisherman of yesterday, for he was wearing a very gay Italian sweater and close-fitting slacks. Stacey approached them diffidently, for certainly they did not look as if they needed anyone else's company, but Lauren had said she had arranged to go sightseeing in Rhodes with a Mr. Hiram Wallace, an American who had some connection with their firm as an influential customer.

'Just a moment, Niko,' said Lauren, drawing Stacey aside and out of his hearing. 'Stacey darling,' she said urgently, 'Niko has asked me to go for a bathe with him and to have lunch. I understand the beaches here are fabulous, and of course Niko knows the best ones to visit.'

Lauren had not wasted much time in furthering this acquaintance now that she knew his true identity.

'But I thought you said we had to go sightseeing with Mr. Wallace, since he's such a good customer of the firm.'

Lauren sighed impatiently.

'Yes, I did, but I was a fool to say I'd go. I really had no intention of spending such a boring day. You'll have to tell him I can't come and that you'll go alone with him.'

'But, Lauren, I couldn't do that.'

'Why not? What does he care so long as he gets some feminine company? Only watch yourself. He's the kind who thinks any girl is fair game. But he can't get very fresh while looking at ruins – or can he? Anyhow, Stacey, you look so innocent that no one in his right mind would make a pass at you. Go on, go and have a good day. And don't argue if he wants to take you out to lunch. Take it from me, he may not be a ship-owner, but he's wealthy enough, and he's important to the firm too, so don't offend him.'

Mr. Hiram Wallace was a rather hardbitten-looking business man who was obviously disappointed when Stacey delivered Lauren's message. She blushed as she said that Lauren was suffering from a migraine brought on by too much sun.

'Well, girlie, we'll have to manage by our own two selves, won't we?' He put a large arm around Stacey and caressed her shoulder, looking a little too appreciatively at her purple sweater. 'What would you like to do, sweetie?' he asked. 'I guess we can hire a car and see the sights of this old town.'

Stacey did not relish the idea of spending the day in a hired car with only Mr. Hiram Wallace for company. In fact she was thoroughly alarmed by the idea.

'I really don't think there's any necessity for that,' she replied. 'I understand a tour has been arranged for the passengers and there's a bus waiting at the jetty. I think we could learn a little more if we went with the rest.'

Hiram Wallace smiled. 'Girlie, you would learn much faster if you came with me. But so be it. The bus it is.'

Lauren had said she must be pleasant to this man because he was one of the firm's customers, but Stacey made up her mind she would get away from him at the first opportunity. Surely she need not stay with him for very long? She would much rather explore this lovely island on her own.

They joined the other tourists and were ushered on to a bus that drove on the climbing road above the modern town in to the old city and up to the palace of the Grand Masters, the old Knights of St. John. Hiram Wallace lit a large cigar which puffed out clouds of smoke in all directions and at the same time he put his arm around Stacey and caressed her shoulders.

Soon they were standing in a sundrenched courtyard with shady arcades and the paving stones echoed to their footsteps as they approached the old palace that had been so skilfully restored during the Italian occupation. In the huge apartments there were beautiful

34

mosaics representing classical myths, and the guide spent an anxious time harrying his party like an anxious sheepdog with disobedient sheep, for he had to guard against anyone stepping on to the precious floor coverings.

Meanwhile Hiram Wallace had met up with some friends whose company seemed more to his liking than that of Stacey and she felt with relief that he would hardly miss her if she tried to slip away. He was laughing loudly with them and, when the crowd was dismissed to find their own way back to the ship after exploring the town, she lingered behind.

Mr. Wallace didn't seem to have missed her yet. He was talking animatedly to another man and a woman. He seemed happy enough without her, so making up her mind swiftly she plunged down one of the side streets. It looked as if it could not have changed much since the Middle Ages and she paused beside a notice leading to a coppersmith's, that invited visitors' inspection of its wares.

In the little alley with its pots of flamboyant geraniums, the sun blazed down, for it was just after noon, and when Stacey walked in to the open doorway of the shop she could not at first see anything, for she was blinded by the sudden change from vivid light to semi-darkness. Gradually the scene cleared and she found herself in a room that was hung with gleaming copper jewellery where she saw a small dark man working at the task of beating the metal whilst another younger man was busy with a customer.

'One moment,' he said. The customer turned to look at her. It was Stavros. She would know that tall figure with its distinctive sculptured features anywhere now.

35

'Why, Miss Grant,' he said, sounding much pleasanter than he had seemed yesterday. 'Are you enjoying your tour of Rhodes?'

'Very much,' said Stacey shyly, for since she had got rid of Mr. Wallace, she was beginning to like it. Then she added a little self-consciously, 'I must thank you for our change of cabin, though really it was not necessary to be so generous. I hope you haven't put yourself to any inconvenience by giving us your quarters?'

'Not at all,' said Stavros, brushing her thanks aside. 'It is the cabin reserved for the women of our family who happen to be travelling on these ships. But in any case, my brother and I are not continuing further on the ship. Our plane awaits us here. We will fly home this evening.'

He picked up a lovely necklace of beaten copper that was styled in an intricate ancient Cretan design.

'And now you can do me a favour by trying on this necklace so that I can see how it looks upon a young woman. I must buy some small trinket to take home with me.'

She bent her head and the young shopkeeper fastened the clasp about her neck. Against her matt creamy skin the goldish bronze metal showed up all its intricate whorls matching the colour of her hair with its spirals of honey-gold curls.

'Beautiful ... *kalliste*,' said the shopkeeper. 'It is made for Madam, quite evidently.'

Stacey was embarrassed that he thought Stavros was buying it for her.

'Do you like it?' asked Stavros. There was something about his dark gaze that confused her still further.

'Of course. Who would not?' she said, trying to hide

her shyness. 'It's quite exquisite.'

Stacey wondered who could be going to receive this lovely gift. He seemed too old to have a fiancée. Was it for his wife? But Lauren, who knew everything, had said he was a widower.

She struggled with the clasp and found herself unable to undo the intricate metal work.

'Let me do it,' said Stavros, and she bent her head and felt his slim brown fingers on her neck unloosening the fastening. Just at that moment, a shadow fell across the sunlit doorway and an American voice said, 'So that's where you're hiding! Someone said they'd seen you disappear up this alley. What about our lunch date, sweetie?' He surveyed the scene with distaste. 'Are you buying that?' he asked. 'I guess you need some help. You mustn't trust these dagoes, you know. They'll sell you anything and always overcharge you.'

Stacey realized that he must think Stavros was a salesman. She flushed in the utmost confusion, not knowing what to say in this unpleasant situation. She felt she wanted to get out of the shop and never see Stavros again. With a murmured apology to him, she joined Hiram Wallace and hurried into the sunlit lane.

'Why in such a hurry, girlie? We could have bought you one of those trinkets you seemed to fancy. I'd like you to know that Hiram B. Wallace is a generous guy, especially when he's out on the town. Now how about joining these buddies of mine for lunch? I arranged to meet them in one of the *tavernas* on the square.'

Stacey was relieved to hear they were not to be alone. They made their way to the restaurant that was filled with tourists from the cruise ship and there they joined another middle-aged man who was accompanied by his

37

wife, a woman dressed in remarkably girlish fashion in spite of her pastel blue hair.

'Aren't you the quiet one?' this lady remarked to Stacey, evidently noticing her withdrawn manner. Stacey made an effort to join in the conversation, but found it difficult. Her quiet voice could not be heard above the raucous conversation of the tourists, the clatter of plates and the sound of bouzouki music coming from a corner of the *taverna*. She felt deeply ashamed that she should have appeared ill-mannered to Stavros. In spite of something forbidding about his manner, he had helped her yesterday by transporting her to Mykonos and today by ordering a change of cabin, and his attitude towards her had been much kinder in the shop when she had tried on the necklace. But when Mr. Wallace had been so rude, her only thought had been to get away from the scene.

'Penny for them,' shouted Mr. Wallace. 'What are you drinking, girlie? I stick to Vichy water in these parts. My doctor said never to drink the wine – my ulcer, you understand.'

The other two were drinking the cloudy ouzo with many exclamations of distaste, but Stacey was served with lemonade made deliciously from fresh-pressed fruit. For a while she felt refreshed, but when the waiter came for their order and Mr. Wallace began to grumble loudly about the Greek food, she felt she could stand no more. The noise, the heat and the smell of cooking food all combined to give her a headache. She turned to him and told him that she did not want any lunch but thought she would return to the ship because she was not feeling well.

The American lady produced some tablets from her

bag and she was forced to take them, while Mr. Wallace made a halfhearted attempt to offer to accompany her, but she refused him, assuring him that she knew the way and would be all right. All she needed was some fresh air. He seemed, if anything, relieved that she was going. Obviously she did not fit in with the other company and he was quite happy now he was with some of his own kind.

She walked for some time before she decided to sit down on the grass. She was some way above the town and could see the ramparts and the deep blue sea below. What should she do now? she thought. It seemed a pity to go back to the ship so early. There was so much to see, and yet she was very weary and it would be difficult to find her way around the island alone. She sat enjoying the sun, which was deliciously warm without being too hot. On this grassy slope she was surrounded by red poppies and other flowers. Her headache had gone, but the tablets the American lady had provided had made her feel sleepy and before she realized it she had drowsed into a deep contented sleep, her head on the jacket at her side.

She was awakened by someone shaking her shoulder a little roughly. 'Miss Grant, are you all right?' For a moment she could not imagine where she was, and then realized that it was Stavros who had her by the arm.

'Yes,' she answered confusedly. 'How silly of me! I must have gone to sleep.'

'Why are you alone? Where are your friends?'

'My friends?'

She still felt confused and muzzy from the effects of the tablets and the sleep in the sun.

'The American gentleman.'

39

Was it her imagination or was there a slightly quizzical intonation over the word?

'I left them having lunch,' she said, freshly embarrassed by the recollection of the scene in the shop. 'I had a headache and it was rather hot and noisy in the restaurant.'

He smiled and looked a little more approving.

'So. It is a woman's privilege always to plead the excuse of a headache. Is that not so? And now, what is your intention?'

'I suppose I should make my way back to the ship.'

'But the ship does not sail until evening. Surely you would like to see some more of the island?'

'I would, of course. But I hardly like to go around by myself, and I'm too late for the afternoon excursion arranged for the passengers.'

He hesitated. It was the first time she had seen him do this, for he seemed always so sure of his own mind. Then he evidently made a decision.

'If you would like to come with me, I could take you to see Lindos. I feel I owe you that for the poor treatment you received on one of our ships.'

She felt embarrassed that he had thought it necessary to take her anywhere.

'Oh, no,' she hastened to disclaim his statement. 'I couldn't put you to so much trouble.'

'No trouble. It would be a pleasure, Miss Grant. And if you have any doubts about my intentions, please let me assure you that I have a very trustworthy chauffeur with me who is the soul of . . . how do you say in English . . . rectitude. You will be quite safe, I assure you.'

She found herself being taken firmly by the arm and walked across the grass towards the waiting car. There was a uniformed chauffeur at the wheel of the silver-grey Rolls. Her will, never very powerful against some-one more determined, seemed to have vanished and she regarded the car with mingled sensations of trepidation and delight.

'I can't miss the ship again,' she protested half-heartedly.

'And you will not,' Stavros assured her, 'I promise you.'

How odd! She felt she could rely upon his word. Was she foolish to accept this invitation? But it was so tempt-ing. It was too late now to turn back. She found herself sinking back into the comfortable seat of the powerful car as it drove down narrow streets amongst the flat-roofed houses of the old city. Below she could see the calm blue waters and near the harbour the minarets of mosques and the sails of windmills.

Rhodes with its almost tropical vegetation, its palm trees and flaunting bougainvilleas, was a complete con-trast to the dry white starkness of the island they had visited before. And as they left the town behind and drove along the tarred road, the land looked fertile and the houses were surrounded by groves of oranges and olive trees with here and there vines supported upon trellises. The small villages they passed were typi-cally Greek, she thought, with the old women in black leading donkeys along the road and the men sitting hav-ing a drink in front of the *tavernas*.

'So you missed lunch?' asked Stavros.

'Yes, but please don't worry about that.'

'But I need it myself,' and he gave instructions to the driver.

Soon they drew up at a country inn, and the welcoming proprietor showed them into a square enclosed courtyard where they sat in the shade of a pergola of vines.

'Will you allow me to order?' asked Stavros, and Stacey willingly assented.

She looked across at her companion and reflected that he also had a kind of charm even if it was less instantly discernible than Niko's. His expression was set in sombre lines and the classical curving lips gave a haughty cast to his face, but his aquiline features were altogether distinguished. How could she not have realized yesterday that he was so aristocratic? He sensed her regard and smiled, and with this his whole face seemed more attractive.

As he discussed the meal with the portly tavern owner, he became more animated. His haughty expression had vanished and he laughed and joked with the man, speaking all the time in colloquial Greek. Soon plates were placed before them with juicy slices of melon, very cool and refreshing after the heat of the journey.

'This is *karpouzi*,' explained Stavros. 'I hope you will like it.'

The clear cold wine that was poured into Stacey's glass was a pale golden green. It was very light, he assured her. He would not give a young girl anything too strong, he said. Suddenly she felt safe with him. The slight trepidation she had felt at her own rashness in accepting his invitation had disappeared. If this had been Niko with whom she was on her way to Lindos she would have been a little apprehensive, for he was obviously an accomplished philanderer. But with this older man she felt no fears of that nature, only a little alarm

42

that she would say the wrong thing or displease him in some way, for he had impressed her yesterday as being rather impatient.

But now he chatted easily about Greece and the islands, putting her at her ease with the practised manner of someone used to dealing with all kinds of people. The melon was followed by *souvlakia*, small pieces of lamb served on skewers which were laid on a bed of shredded lettuce and served with quarters of lemon.

'These taste wonderful,' Stacey said, and Stavros looked pleased.

'Nothing could be more simple,' he said. 'It is the usual *taverna* food, lamb grilled over wood smoke.'

'That must be what gives it its distinctive taste,' said Stacey. 'And the taste of herbs. What kind are used?'

'Usually a kind of herb that grows wild on the mountains ... it is called *rigani* ... what would that be? Origanum, literally in English "Joy of the mountains".'

The strange but tasty food, the simplicity of the courtyard in the country *taverna*, the easy manners of her companion, all put Stacey at her ease and she talked more freely than she usually did, chatting away happily, not hindered by Lauren's more exotic presence and her disapproval of what she called Stacey's gaucheness.

The proprietor of the inn insisted that Stacey try his *paklava* next, but Stavros was content to sit with a cup of black coffee and a glass of water while she ate the crisp flaky confection dripping with honey and filled with a delectable filling of almonds. She was served with coffee too, but could scarcely repress a shudder when she tasted its bitterness coming as a shock after the sweetness of the *paklava*.

Stavros saw this and was amused.

'Our coffee seemed to be an acquired taste, like ouzo and retsina. The water we drink with it takes away the bitterness a little, you will find.'

Soon they were on their way again and now the road began to climb upwards, winding close to the grape-blue sea. On the breeze from the sharp-edged hills came the smell of wild thyme and the rigani that had flavoured their lunch. The road became steeper, then just as suddenly dipped into a valley. Stavros told the chauffeur to halt and in front of them was the great craggy headland, and there, faintly seen in the distance, were the ancient walls of the citadel.

They left the car in the small town in an open space where a fountain played under a plane tree. The town seemed unreal to Stacey, so much was it like a modern landscape painting, the white houses all cubes and squares, the electric lights in the streets hanging in primitive nakedness from standards looped with sagging wires.

'The path is uphill. What do you say? Shall we walk or ride donkeys?' asked Stavros. Stacey looked at the mild-eyed donkeys with their owners, who were old ladies dressed in black with dark kerchiefs on their heads. She saw some of them urging the little animals up the narrow alleys, exhorting them with beating of sticks and an occasional kick. Although the donkeys seemed well used to it even to the point of indifference, she chose to walk, and they progressed along the streets that were paved with black and white pebbles, and lined with small shops designed to tempt the tourist, shoe shops like dark little caves in the wall, their wares of Greek

44

sandals hanging on strings outside and windows ranged with pottery, terra-cotta colour with delicate friezes, coloured woven rugs and goatskins of creamy hair.

The streets were so narrow that sometimes they had to stand aside as the donkeys stamped their way past. When this happened, Stavros took her arm as he drew her aside. On one occasion, close to him now, she glanced quickly at his face. He had such an unreadable expression that she could not tell whether he was enjoying her company or not. It was good of him, she supposed, to take the trouble to show her something of the island, for he must be an extremely busy man. And why had he done it? It must have been in order to make up in some way for their difficulties on board ship. For he could hardly have any other interest in her. The thing that reassured her about accompanying him was that he spoke to her as he would, she thought, to a child. He obviously did not regard her as a grown-up woman. In any case he was so much older than she was, much older than Niko.

At the foot of the steps which ascended to the Acropolis was the prow of an ancient ship sculptured into the rock. The narrow staircase clung first to the rock and then to the ramparts of the old fortification leading to a castle gateway. And now there were more stairs, and it seemed to Stacey as if she were climbing a staircase to heaven, for there was nothing to be seen but a vista of deep blue sky. But ascending further she saw the columns of a temple, sparkling on its airy height. Stavros took her arm as they stood on the edge of the parapet around it, for the red rock fell vertically towards the clear sea, three hundred and fifty feet below. In the luminous light she could see the great sweep of turquoise water dotted with tiny silver islands.

'You like it?' asked Stavros, shouting to make his voice heard against the sound of the rushing wind. She nodded breathlessly, caught in enforced intimacy with this stranger as he held her still against the swaying force of air. She knew she would never forget this afternoon, the golden columns of the temple upon the massive rock and the flashing brilliance of sunlight upon the sea below.

They seemed to have descended to another world when they came down to the white town with its harbour of blue water, where they sat at a table near the beach that had brightly coloured boats drawn up on to the sand, and drank fresh orange juice.

'I'm so grateful to you for this lovely afternoon,' Stacey said shyly. 'Now I can understand what fascination the Greek islands have for people.'

She was thinking of Colin and her expression grew soft and tender. Stavros was watching her more closely than she realized.

'Are you thinking of anyone in particular?' he asked. 'Have you friends living here in the islands?'

'A friend,' she admitted, confessing more than usual because she was touched by the lovely day she had spent and the luminous radiance of the late afternoon light falling softly upon the sea.

'And where is he? For I see by your expression that this is a young man you speak of?'

'He's Lauren's brother,' she said, trying now to make it seem of little importance to her. 'He lives on a small island. Ships don't usually call there. But we've arranged that a launch should call for us when we arrive within a few miles of it. It's called Paxados. Do you

46

know of it?'

His expression hardly seemed to have changed and yet a flicker of some kind had passed over his dark face.

'Yes, I know it. And the name of your friend?'

'Colin Hamilton. He's gone there to write a book. I haven't heard how it's progressing, but it's wonderful good fortune that we were sent to Athens in connection with Lauren's work and can now go to visit him.'

'Does Mr. Hamilton know you are coming?'

Stacey was getting used to the national trait of insatiable curiosity. Everyone she had met in Athens had asked innumerable questions. So now she replied, 'We wrote a letter to him but have had no reply. And we sent a telegram just before we left in order to make sure he knew about it.'

'Well, I hope you enjoy your stay on Paxados as much as you expect to.'

'I'm sure we shall. Colin says it's fabulous.'

'It depends very much on the personality, of course, whether you enjoy life on a Greek island or not. They are all different. You must not expect Paxados to be like Rhodes, for instance.'

'Oh, no, I won't,' said Stacey eagerly. 'But I'm sure we're going to love it.'

Anywhere where Colin is will be wonderful to me, she thought.

'Have you ever been there?' she asked curiously.

'Yes. I have a house on the island. It is a house the family use for holidays. We call it the Citadel of Swallows because year after year the swallows return to nest in a ruined temple close by and in the eaves of the house itself. We usually spend a vacation there in spring or

47

summer. In the winter we live in Athens. I will be flying to Paxados very shortly. We may meet again, Miss Grant.'

He had been so likeable the whole afternoon. She felt disappointed that the severe manner she had first noticed seemed to have returned. When they said goodbye he cut short her flustered attempts to thank him. After all, perhaps he had not enjoyed the excursion as much as she herself had.

CHAPTER THREE

AND now at last their cruise was over and they were approaching Paxados in a small boat. Each island they had seen seemed to have its own individual character and no two had been alike. Mykonos and Delos had been remarkable for their lack of vegetation and flatness, but this island, although small, seemed to have hills towards its centre covered with pine trees and some buildings. There was a quay with a circle of buildings like white sugar cubes in a crescent shape around the blue water, but higher up there were roofs of tiles in that wonderful brick-red colour that seemed more characteristic of an Italian landscape.

Stacey strained her eyes to catch a glimpse of Colin. She could not see any sign of movement on the quayside beside the half circle of white houses, but he must be there. It would be wonderful to see him again after all these months. Letters were so unsatisfactory, but she was sure that when she saw him again she would feel again the thrilling awareness that she had known when she first came to London and he had paid her so much attention when she had not expected it.

Her heart was beating fast and she stole a glance in the small mirror of her handbag. She hoped she would look beautiful to him, and she looked in some alarm at her tawny gold hair that was dishevelled by the sea wind, not realizing that the curling strands looked charming framing her heart-shaped face with its creamy skin and pansy-brown eyes.

But when they arrived at the steps leading on to a small jetty, Stacey's heart sank and she could scarcely conceal her bitter disappointment. Colin was not there. Paxados drowsed in the afternoon sun. The shutters of the buildings were closed. A few seagulls looking for fish and a white cat basking in the sun were the only living things visible.

'What do we do now?' asked Lauren, yawning as if the torpid scene had affected her too. 'How like Colin to leave us to find our own way to his place. I wonder where we can get a taxi?'

'He may not have got our letter or telegram,' Stacey suggested reasonably, although her whole body seemed to be trembling with emotion and it was difficult not to show this.

'I suppose not. I wonder if he has a phone. Stacey, be an angel and see if you can find a phone in that café over there and if not, ask about a taxi.'

With that, Lauren sat down on her bright-red suit-case in the shade of a wall and lighting a cigarette temporarily lost interest in the proceedings. It had been like this all the time. She was very good at giving orders and expected them to be carried out however difficult Stacey found it.

Walking across the cobblestones, Stacey arrived at the café, but when she tried it the door was locked. Inside she could see an enormously fat man sleeping soundly, his head on his arms at a table, and she rattled the door, but there was no response.

She stood uncertainly and looked up and down the street, and, as if in answer to her wish, saw a movement in the shade of a building. What a disappointment! It was a small goat, not unlike the one she had seen on

Delos. Oh, but there was someone with it. A very small boy, it was true, but perhaps she could ask him. He came strolling towards her, the goat following at his heels. His large brown eyes showed a lively curiosity and they sparkled with quick intelligence.

'Allo, allo,' he greeted her. 'You American, hey?'

With his feet apart planted sturdily upon the ground and his thin body, firm and supple, he looked a picture of independence.

'British,' she answered, thinking that probably his English was limited to a few words and it was no use trying to say too much. 'Taxi?' she suggested hopefully. 'Auto?'

To her surprise the small boy laughed heartily.

'No taxi here,' he said. His curly black head was flung back and he burst into another delightful peal of laughter. 'No cars here. No roads.'

This was a problem. 'Colin Hamilton,' she said tentatively. 'His house?'

The boy looked keenly interested.

'You want Kyrios Colin?'

'Yes, we have come all the way from England to visit him.'

He threw back his head and laughed again.

'All the girls, they like Colin.'

She was rather nettled by this statement, but then chided herself, because after all he was only a child and could not understand he had hurt her.

'How can we get to his house? We have luggage with us.'

'I will fix,' said the small dark boy.

He tied his goat to a bollard on the quay and disappeared down a side street from which he emerged presently with four donkeys and another youngster slightly older than himself. Lauren's face was a study when Stacey returned with her retinue of small boys and donkeys.

'You don't mean that this is the only means of transport?'

'Apparently it is,' Stacey confirmed.

'In that case I'll stay here while you make some preparatory investigation. I'll sit in the shade on that verandah until the café opens. It must open some time during the afternoon.'

'But, Lauren . . .' Stacey knew it was useless to remonstrate. When Lauren made up her mind to a course of action, she could not be persuaded away from it. She wondered how she would be able to cope with the boys, the donkeys and the luggage on her own, and yet she could not help being glad that she was to meet Colin alone.

As things turned out she need not have worried, for the boy who had come to her assistance was taking everything in hand in a very capable way, giving instructions to the other one, although the second boy appeared to be a little older.

'What is your name?' she asked of the first one.

'Socrates,' he said, and then observing her smile, 'One calls me Sox. And he is Dimitraki.'

Dimitraki evidently did not have any English, for he was silent and rather solemn, loading suitcases on each side of the donkeys like panniers, whereas Socrates or Sox was voluble and vivacious and evidently good at ordering someone else to do the work.

He helped her on to the unloaded donkey with the utmost courtesy and after it had been given a smart slap it trotted briskly along the quay and turned down a side street which led in turn to a path up the hillside. It evidently knew the way, for it needed no guiding, and with Sox shouting something that sounded like 'Opsa!', Stacey held the reins loosely as she bounced up and down. When she became used to the motion, it was not unenjoyable. Here and there along the path were small white houses, sometimes surrounded by a small grove of olive trees. She saw white goats grazing and wondered what had happened to the little kid belonging to Sox, but then saw that he had strapped it on to one of the donkeys and it was proceeding up the hill in this fashion, bleating plaintively all the way.

Below them the bay opened out in a curve of blue water and beside them the meadows were covered with bright poppies and yellow gorse and there was a smell of grass and thyme and sometimes faintly on the breeze a more elusive fragrance of the pine trees on the upper slopes. High up Stacey could see the small ruin of golden pillars and not far from this there was a house bigger than the cottages they had passed. She could see red tiles and a sweep of white staircase above the trees.

But now Sox was giving more orders and the donkeys slowed down. Standing by itself above a small inlet of blue ocean below, there was a white cottage, no different it seemed from all the others. Stacey's heart beat fast. Surely now she would see Colin. But the door was shut and Sox, who evidently knew his way around, was searching behind a waterbutt to find the key with which he opened the stable type of front door.

It opened on to a square small room of whitewashed brick with the floor of red tiles. The furniture was of the simplest, a sofa made of stone built in against the wall and upholstered with woven gold linen cushions and beside this on the deal table an oil lamp made from a green glass demi-john. On another table near the window there was an open typewriter. But where was Colin?

'Kyrios Hamilton?' she asked the small Socrates.

'Is at house,' said Sox, pointing upwards towards the higher slopes. 'Kyrios Colin work at my house.'

Stacey was puzzled. How could Colin be working at someone else's house? Unless it was a quieter place for writing. But this place seemed quiet enough. At that moment she was conscious that there was another person standing watching her from the doorway. She started violently, but it was not Colin. Only a girl of about her own age.

She was dressed in black in a long dress and head-shawl, and her colouring was dark too. Black hair in smooth blackbird's wings sprang from a centre parting above large black eyes that had something still and yet piercing about them as she gazed at Stacey. She spoke in an angry tone to Sox and he replied just as sharply, as if he were telling her to go. But she flounced into the room, looking, Stacey thought, not so much like a Greek girl as like an actress in 'Carmen', and opening an inlaid box, helped herself to a cigarette with deliberate insolence of manner as if to convey to Stacey that she was very much at home in Colin's house.

Stacey felt at a loss. 'Who is she?' she asked Sox.

Sox gave the girl a glance of dislike.

'Her name Chrysoula. She clean this house for Colin, but not now. Colin not want her now and she is cross.'

A torrent of Greek from Chrysoula followed this

statement. Stacey thought it likely that she knew a little English if she had been working for Colin. He had not mentioned in his letters that he had someone to clean for him. But then he did not worry about such mundane details when writing to her. But just then there was an interruption.

'What pleasure! We meet again, Miss Stacey.'

Niko stood in the doorway, smiling and holding out his hands. It was such a relief to Stacey to see someone she knew and even more someone who understood English properly that she felt almost as if he were an old friend. He spoke sharply to Chrysoula and she flounced out of the door muttering sulkily.

'So my young relative found you. That is good.'

'Your relative?'

'Socrates. He lives with us when he is not roaming the island. Did you not recognize the goat we brought from Delos? Flavia strayed away when we went for an excursion there. But no matter. Lauren telephoned from the *kafenion*. I have sent a mule and trap to fetch her and she should arrive any moment. Then I will take you both up to the house. Our cousin Sophia has invited you to a meal. She is anxious to meet you.'

His smile was as charming as Stacey remembered. How good it seemed to have someone to organize things for them. But where was Colin?

He seemed to sense her anxiety, for he said, 'Colin is at the house. He sends his apologies and will see you at lunch time. Did he not tell you he is engaged in some work of cataloguing the family's large collection of ancient Greek relics and writings? And he coaches this naughty one when he can get him to stay indoors.'

Colin had never mentioned this. Strange – Stacey had

thought all along that he was engaged solely upon writing the book.

Niko gave instructions to Sox who together with Dimitraki went down the hill to meet Lauren. Eventually she appeared in a small cart drawn by a milk-white mule, its forehead adorned with a string of blue beads. Her sulkiness had disappeared with the advent of Niko, but she looked with some horror at the simple living arrangements of the cottage.

'I've found out,' she said, 'that there's no hotel on this island and Colin appears to have only one bed. Heaven knows where we're to sleep!'

'Don't worry,' said Niko. 'Doubtless we can arrange something. And now for lunch.'

As they ascended the path the scene changed and instead of grassy slopes there were pine trees that showed between their trunks glimpses of misty-blue air. Somewhere there was the sound of running water and, high up on the slopes, the tinkle of sheep's bells. The donkeys speeded up as if they were pleased that they were reaching their destination. And there was the house, large and low and made of mellow stone, with above it, high on the headland, the golden pillars that Stacey had glimpsed from the ship.

There were two broad flights of marble steps leading to the huge carved front door, and as they approached this door opened and a woman of about forty came out. She was plump and comfortable yet tall and in a way imposing in the dignity of her carriage. Not by any means pretty, she still had a rather regal air as she stood with arms outstretched in a welcoming gesture at the top of the marble stairs. Her face was round and creased with laughter lines and her hair was parted in the middle and caught up in a knot at her neck. Behind her stood two maids in black with white aprons and each carried a tray.

'Here is Sophia,' said Niko. 'Now you must observe the Greek custom of welcome to the house. Sophia is a great one for keeping to the old traditions.'

Upon the one tray were two glasses of iced water and on the other some small dishes of candied fruit and cherry jam together with two long silver spoons. When Niko had made the introductions, Sophia bowed graciously and gestured towards the trays.

'You are most welcome to our house,' she said, and gestured to the trays, instructing them to take the spoons, help themselves to the fruit and dip it in the iced water, then eat it and finally drink the water. In any other surroundings, Stacey would have expected Lauren to scoff at this, but she was obviously impressed with the large house and the family circumstances.

'And now,' said Sophia, 'come in and we will have an aperitif, which will be more to your liking, yes?'

They followed her through the carved door which led in to a large hall of shining red tiles. There were doors on each side leading into living-rooms, but, at the back of the hall, was a door of glass that led into a sheltered courtyard which was the centre of the house. The floor was paved in marble of black and white and there was a pergola of vines stretching around the quadrangle and making it look like a shadowy cloister. Bright geraniums of vivid pink grew in ornamental urns and in the middle a fountain sprayed water with the cool sound of tinkling chimes.

A serving man brought a trolley of drinks and they sat at the white wrought-iron table in the leafy-dappled shade. Stacey thought it was good to rest after the unusual experiences of the morning, the climb uphill with the donkeys and the disappointment that Colin was not there to meet them.

But where was Colin now? Surely he knew they had arrived? Sophia seemed to sense her uneasiness, for she said, 'You are thinking we keep your friend hard at work when you wish so much to see him. It is true he works hard here, but that is his own choice. He spends much more time here than he really owes us. But I will send now to see what has happened to him.'

She spoke to the manservant who whispered a reply. Nothing, thought Stacey, could ruffle Sophia's calm dignity, but she looked very slightly disturbed by the news he had conveyed.

'I am mistaken. It seems Colin is not in the library. He and Alexandra have gone for a swim before lunch. Alexandra is my daughter. She is the only young girl in our household and I am afraid we all spoil her. She gets a little bored here and is always longing for Athens.'

There was the sound of laughter as two people stood framed in an archway that looked towards the deep-blue sea. They were, it seemed, unaware that anyone was watching them, for they were absorbed in each other's company and the girl was looking up at her companion with a radiant teasing smile. She was wearing a brief flame-coloured bikini that flattered the dark-honey colour of her lithe young body and there were bright-gold sandals on her feet.

There seemed a slight sharpness in Sophia's voice as she called hurriedly, 'Come and meet my guests, Alexandra. Shame on you for taking Colin away when he must have been longing to stay here to greet his friend

58

and his sister from England!'

Alexandra pouted, then laughed.

'You enjoyed your swim. Don't deny it, Colin.'

She came swiftly across to the table, her graceful walk showing off her lovely limbs. She seemed very young, but more mature than an English girl would have been. She was, Stacey thought, about sixteen or possibly seventeen, very beautiful in a dark vibrant way.

'Put on your wrap, my dear,' Sophia said.

The girl made a little face but obeyed her mother, wrapping the white garment tightly around her slender hips. Colin had followed more slowly and now stood smiling down at them both. Lauren jumped up and flung her arms around him and they kissed, but Stacey hung back. She had hoped their first meeting would take place when they were alone. If only he had been at the cottage! She felt that this was embarrassing, to meet him again after all these months in front of strangers.

He was laughing after his encounter with Lauren. How brown he looked, beautifully tanned. He must spend a lot of time out of doors, for it was only springtime as yet. His brown hair sprang in lively waves from his forehead and his grey eyes sparkled with good health. Certainly the island life seemed to agree with him, for he was more handsome than ever.

'And Stacey?' He turned to her and kissed her a little hesitantly. Perhaps he too felt that it would have been better if they had had their first meeting alone. She noticed that Alexandra was regarding them with great interest. She looked especially at Lauren as if analysing her clothes and her looks. Then she looked back at Colin and seemed to wish to read his feelings from his expression.

'This is a lovely surprise,' he said.

'But didn't you know we were coming?' demanded Lauren.

'Only a little while ago, when they phoned through to tell us about your telegram. You have to make allowances for our communications. Here we're not in Athens or London.'

Explanations followed while they all drank a kind of fruit punch. Another servant approached with a trolley of every kind of snack, small fried octopus, mussels, small clams and scampi together with small rolls of vine leaves wrapped around a delicious mixture of meat, rice and spices. This must be the way the Greeks served lunch in an informal way, thought Stacey, for she could not imagine they were to have more food after this. Lauren and Sophia and Niko seemed to be doing most of the talking. Alexandra was still busy with her contemplation of Lauren, and Stacey was quiet, because now that she had at last met Colin there seemed nothing to say. It was exasperating to have to sit here exchanging social chitchat, charming as these people were, when she was anxious to know all about Colin, and to become up to date with his present life and the progress of his 'best-seller'.

'Oh, that will be absolutely wonderful, won't it, Stacey?' she heard Lauren say, enthusiastically. She had not heard a word of the previous conversation and did not know what they had been talking about.

'I'm sorry,' she said. 'I didn't hear. I must have been thinking of something else.'

'Stacey is given to daydreams,' Lauren explained. 'Mrs. Demetrios ... Sophia ... (this as Sophia murmured a protest) ... has suggested that we should stay here.'

Stacey was startled. How could they stay with these people whom they hardly knew?

'Oh, no, you can't mean it. Surely we can't put you to so much trouble,' she protested.

'I would not ask you if I did not mean it. Allow us to show you something of our famous Greek hospitality. There is not a hotel on the island and the cottages are very simple. You will be so much more comfortable here. I assure you it will be no trouble to have guests. We are delighted to meet new people here. And we have many servants and can always hire more from amongst the village people.'

Stacey was disarmed. 'Well, perhaps for a few days.'

'I insist that you stay until you have seen a Greek Easter festival. To us it is the most important festival in the Christian calendar, as important as Christmas is to the English.'

'That will be fabulous, won't it, Stacey?'

Lauren was obviously most anxious that they should stay. And of course Stacey was too in her innermost heart. It would be wonderful to spend some time near Colin. She looked his way, anxious to surprise some glance which would be more personal than he had given her up to now, but he was having some little teasing joke with Alexandra. Stacey felt a pang of dismay. But she assured herself that she was being foolish. Alexandra was a charming child.

'And now that has been decided, I will ring and tell the servants they can serve lunch,' declared Sophia.

So this had not been their lunch?

Sophia looked around. 'Now where is Stavros?' she asked.

'I forgot to tell you. We passed him on our way from the beach. He was supervising some business with the young grapes and said we should not wait lunch for him. He will come in later.'

The servants arrived with loaded trays and Stacey was glad she could boast a healthy appetite when she was handed a large helping of *moussaka* and this was followed by an enormous choice of cheeses together with fresh peaches and black grapes that had been flown, Sophia said, from Africa.

'We live very simply, when we are in our island home,' she explained.

An Irish setter loped in through the archway, its pelt glinting red-gold in the sun, its plumy tail waving vigorously.

'Stavros must be coming,' said Sophia, 'for here is Apollo.'

What a lovely name for a dog that seems made of golden light, thought Stacey.

And here comes Stavros. He looked younger somehow than he had done that day at Rhodes, for then he had been formally dressed in a dark suit, but now he was wearing light-brown slacks and suede jacket of russet brown. It was true, thought Stacey, recalling her first impression, that he was good-looking.

This had been overshadowed a little by her later impression that he was someone a little awe-inspiring. But now as he strode across to join the group he seemed a person completely at home and at ease, and Stacey saw some of Niki's charm in the smile with which he greeted them.

'So we meet once more,' he said.

There was an empty chair next to Stacey and she had

been hoping Colin would notice this and make a move to sit next to her, but now Stavros took it and a servant opened a bottle of German lager and handed it to him. He regarded the sparkling golden drink with appreciation.

'Will you excuse me if I drink this, Miss Grant? I have been looking forward to it for the last hour. For spring the sun is very hot in the vineyards.'

He took a long swallow. He had discarded his jacket and was wearing an Italian cotton-knit sweater of olive green, and she noticed that in spite of his apparent slenderness he had powerful shoulders and strong arms.

'So you have met your friend, Colin,' he said, and to Stacey's surprise he gave her a teasing smile.

'You didn't tell me you knew him,' she reproached him.

'I thought it better not. If he had not mentioned to you that he knew us, I thought it would be better that you found out yourself.'

It was puzzling, thought Stacey. Why had Colin not mentioned that he was friendly with the Demetrios family? But then his letters had been slight of late, just assuring her that he was well and getting on famously with the book and that he thought of her a lot and longed to see her. With that she looked across at him again. For someone who had written so consistently that he was longing to see her, he did not seem to be making much effort to be near her. But then perhaps he did not want to embarrass her before people who were strangers.

'Stavros, I've persuaded Lauren and Stacey to stay here with us,' said Sophia. 'It will be much more comfortable than hiring a cottage or some rooms in the village and it will be company for Alexandra.'

Did Alexandra need any other company? thought Stacey. She seemed to be completely absorbed in Colin. They were talking and chatting together, ignoring the rest of the company. She saw that Stavros gave a quick frown and said something in an undertone to Sophia, and she was sure that he did not really approve of Sophy's having asked them to stay. Sophia, however, replied calmly and he turned with a smile to the two girls and said, 'That is good, that you are to be our guests. It is lonely here for Alexandra, I agree.'

Alexandra frowned. 'Oh, Stavros, I am quite happy here. You know that.'

'What is this now?' he said, frowning a little, but then smiling in that teasing way. 'When we came here you made a big fuss and said you did not want to leave Athens.'

She smiled, her brown cheeks dimpling, and leaned across to touch his cheek with her hand.

'Darling Stavros, that was ages ago – at least two weeks. And now the good weather has come and I had forgotten how good it is to swim here.'

Stavros looked at her, his expression a little severe.

'So. I am glad to hear this. It seems the sacred ikon in the church below must have worked some miracle, for I still remember how you fought with your poor mother and said you hated the idea of coming here.'

A languorous afternoon feeling seemed to be settling on the company, and Sophia arose and said she was going to take her rest but that she would instruct the servants to prepare their rooms. Doubtless they would like to have some talk with Colin. She would arrange that their luggage should be fetched from the house.

64

Stavros had risen with Sophia, saying he had some phone calls to make to Athens. He turned to Stacey.

'We will meet again, Miss Grant. Enjoy your stay on our Greek island. Remember the French proverb, everything passes, everything changes in life.'

Now what did he mean by that? thought Stacey, as she watched him walk away, his long lithe stride making the distance across the courtyard seem short. The swallows were flying in and out of the eaves in the upper storey, their twittering making a continuous sound that seemed to give a soft background to the peaceful afternoon.

'A penny for them.'

Now when she least expected it, she found herself alone with Colin, for Alexandra had gone to change and Lauren was laughing and talking with Niko some distance away.

He was laughing down into her eyes with the same sparkling charm that she had known in London.

'Well, and how's little Stacey?' he asked.

She was somehow jarred by his question. It put her on a different footing than she had expected. It seemed to place her in the same category as the young Alexandra. But she pulled herself together. She must not imagine things when she had not even spoken to him alone yet.

'I'm well,' she said. 'Oh, Colin, it is lovely to be here. I'm so looking forward to hearing all about your book.'

'Well ... yes. But we'll talk about that later. It's lovely to see you, Stacey – and looking as charming as ever. One can see you haven't been unhappy without me.'

She was confused and did not know how to reply to this. How could she say that she had been hoping and dreaming of this meeting for many lonely months? And now this man who stood in front of her, so good-looking, so attractive, seemed from the expression in his eyes to be almost a stranger.

CHAPTER FOUR

FOR a little while they had spoken together, but of nothing that seemed important to Stacey, and now this stranger whom she could hardly reconcile with her dream of her beloved Colin turned to her and said, 'Stacey, my dear, will you mind if I leave you now? It's a great nuisance just as you've arrived, but I was interrupted this morning and I still have some work to do in the library. I'll see you this evening because Sophia has asked me to stay for dinner, and after that we'll have a long talk and you can tell me all about yourself. I'm looking forward to getting news of London.'

Stacey made no attempt to keep him with her, yet she could not help reflecting that if he had not been interrupted this morning by the necessity to have a pre-lunch swim, he could possibly have had the talk with her now. Oh, but she must not think such things. It was only because she was tired and disappointed that her meeting with Colin seemed such an anticlimax to all her hopes. She was sure that when they had had time to talk everything would sort itself out and they would be back on their old footing.

Lauren had disappeared, presumably to rest, but Stacey was too timid to investigate where their rooms were. She tried to rest upon a chaise-longue in the courtyard, but after half an hour with her mind still in a turmoil she felt very restless. She was wondering rather forlornly what to do next when there was a gay whistling and Sox came hopping across the quadrangle and beckoned to her.

'You want to come?' he asked. 'We go to bring your cases. You like another ride on donkey, yes?'

It would be something to occupy her. Anything would be better than trying to rest and brooding over Colin. She nodded agreement to Sox and he smiled very joyously and ran off to fetch the donkeys.

She had realized by now that Sox was much more fluent in England than she had at first thought, and now that he had become friendly with her he chatted very happily, only occasionally coming out with some quaint phrase or hesitating, furious with himself for being stuck over a word. Stacey chose to walk down rather than ride and Dimitraki went ahead leading the donkeys, while Sox conversed politely with her, evidently feeling this was his duty as her host.

The two dark little donkeys trotted quickly down the slope and every now and then Dimitraki called, '*Siga, parakalo*,' which Sox informed her conveyed to the donkeys that they must please go slowly. Stacey repeated that thinking that it seemed like a useful phrase to learn where riding donkeys was concerned.

'They are called Mercedes and Lambrini,' he informed her. 'But donkeys not as good as cars. In Athens, Stavros has beautiful cars, a Rolls from England and a sports car. That one is the best. He does not drive as fast as Niko. Niko is like devil on road.'

'The beads look pretty on the donkeys' brows,' Stacey commented.

'They are to ward off evil eye,' said Sox seriously. 'Some people can look at one and wish bad things. Same with donkeys.'

Stacey was surprised. What an odd mixture went to

68

make up the Greek character! One moment this young boy was discussing modern cars, and next expressing a sincere belief in witchcraft. He seemed, she thought, truly typical of the Greek characteristics she had noticed so far, for he had great charm and vivacity and a kind of quick brilliance. When he grew up she could imagine him being like Niko, all audacity and grace. She was not so sure about Stavros. He seemed more difficult and not so open as Niko, but then he was the head of the family, the elder brother. She could imagine him being disapproving of anything which went against his own ideas. There was something unenlightened, she had heard, about the Greek's attitude to women. The long Turkish occupation seemed to have left its mark. In this modern age the Greek standards were far away from the liberal attitude of British society.

By the side of the road, there was a spring with a stone trough and women were doing washing there. Others wrapped in black shawls led donkeys laden with anything from a mattress to bundles of firewood. Few men were visible and when Stacey commented on this Sox looked surprised and then laughed.

'The men will be at the *kafenion* now playing *tavli*. I think you call the game domino. Why should they do these things when they have wives? In the early morning they fish. In the daytime they rest and drink and play *tavli*.'

Stacey refrained from comment. The men of the island had evidently found an ideal way to live. She was not so sure about the women. But she was nevertheless charmed by the island, the groves of silvery-grey olives, the blinding-white houses, the sea smooth now as pale-blue silk. She could understand its fascination for Colin.

They had come now to the little white house and to Stacey's surprise the door stood open. She could hear voices from within that sounded loud and harsh. She hesitated and said to Sox, 'Wait here. I'll call you when the suitcases are ready.'

He gave her a look, a little more hesitant than his usual direct manner. 'Perhaps you should wait also,' he said. 'Kyrios Colin may not like.'

But Colin was in the library. He could not be here, Stacey thought. The voices had quietened now. Perhaps it was the girl who cleaned the cottage. What was her name? Chrysoula. She might have been talking with some friend, for the Greeks always seemed to sound as if they were arguing when they were just a little livelier than usual. And she must see about the luggage.

With this she approached the open door. The two people in the living-room of the cottage had not heard the sound of her footsteps, for they were absorbed in each other. Colin and Chrysoula were locked in a passionate embrace, and as Stacey recoiled, she saw the girl lean away from him and laugh provocatively as if she felt triumphant that their dispute had ended as she wished. Stacey gasped. There was a physical pain at her heart and she turned to go away, but not before Colin had raised his eyes and looking over the girl's head had seen her in the doorway.

Stacey walked slowly back to Sox and without speaking to him sat on a bench that was placed to overlook the glorious blue-green sea and the coastline with its craggy inlets and foaming waves, but she saw nothing of this. She saw only Chrysoula's triumphant expression as she held Colin in that close embrace. Presently a shadow fell upon her and Colin stood there. She turned and could see the lithe dark-clad figure of Chrysoula striding effortlessly up the hillside, her hips swinging. Every now and again she cast a backward glance and even waved. But Colin made no response. He took Stacey's hands and drawing her up from the bench said as if nothing untoward had happened, 'Stacey, how nice to see you. Do come in and see my house properly.'

He put his arm around her shoulder and drew her inside. She could hardly refuse, especially in front of Sox, who was lying on the sunbaked grass sucking a straw and shouting instructions to Dimitraki who had let the donkeys stray.

The room was as she remembered it, flickering with leafy shadows and yellow sunlight. But it seemed spoiled for her now. Colin seemed to sense her disquiet, for he dropped his hand while still giving her one of those disarming smiles. She walked over to the table, a plain deal one with a small typewriter open upon it. Leaning over to look at the foolscap in it, she saw the page was blank.

'How's the book going, Colin?' she asked, wanting to talk about any subject but the one uppermost in her mind.

'Not too badly,' he said. 'Naturally I don't have much time because the Demetrios family keep me pretty occupied.'

Looking at the typewriter she saw that Chrysoula could not be too particular about cleaning it, for on the keys there was a layer of dust. It had not been touched for a long time.

'But Colin,' she said, 'surely the book should come first. After all, that's the reason why you came here. Don't you remember you were to write your best-seller, and I'm absolutely certain that you can.'

He looked sulky. 'Don't be childish, Stacey. It isn't as easy as that. Besides, the Demetrios family have been good to me, and they pay well too.'

'But I thought you had enough money to live on. You said it wouldn't cost much here.'

She forbore to remind him that she had lent him money, the very small amount of her savings, which, he had assured her, it was better to spend on this project than keeping to help towards their marriage. And he seemed now to have forgotten about it.

He went up to her and ruffled her hair, caressing the nape of her neck where the silky tendrils of honey-gold hair escaped from their knot.

'Stacey, sweet one, surely you haven't turned into a scold? Just make up your mind to enjoy yourself while you're here. Let tomorrow take care of itself. Don't you think you're fortunate to be staying in the Demetrios household? If it hadn't been for my connection with them you would have had to find a cottage to rent and, heaven knows, this one is pretty primitive.'

'It seems to be provided with some home comforts,' she blurted out bitterly.

He laughed, quite unperturbed.

'Chrysoula? Oh, surely, darling, you can't be jealous of her. She's just a little tiger kitten. I was too kind to her at first and now I don't seem to be able to get rid of her.'

'You didn't seem to be making much effort,' said Stacey.

'That? Believe me, it wasn't of my own making.'

He came and took her in his arms, but her senses failed to respond. She merely felt annoyed that he could do this to her when he had so recently been embracing another woman.

'So sorry to interrupt you,' said the voice of Stavros. 'I was passing the cottage and wondered if you were here, Colin. I had something to discuss with you, but see you are pleasantly occupied. Another time will do.'

Stacey was dismayed and embarrassed at being found here with Colin – and especially by Stavros. If it had been Niko she would have passed it off with some joke, but the older man looked most disapproving, she thought. Colin was supposed to be working at the house. Stavros probably thought the two of them had come down here especially to be alone together. How grim he could look with his thin dark face and that sneering curve of the lips. His mouth was certainly not smiling now.

'I'm going immediately,' she said to him. 'I'll call Sox to help take the luggage.'

She went outside without a backward glance at Colin. She felt furious and deeply disturbed. But she told Sox and Dimitraki that they could bring the bags and she would see them later. Again she set out on her way up the steep path, the way she had taken earlier so full of hopes and dreams about Colin and their meeting. Now she must face the fact that Colin, the man she had hoped to marry, was a philanderer. And yet perhaps there was some explanation. Perhaps now that she had arrived everything would be as it had been before. She must not be too harsh in her judgment of him. After all, she had always known he was very attractive to other women. She must learn to be philosophical if she intended to spend her life with him. So she argued with herself as she climbed higher and higher up the path. She could see the donkeys far below being led by Sox and Dim-itraki. There really had been no need for her to come at all. How she wished she hadn't!

When she reached the entrance to the house, she did not feel like facing the others yet, especially Lauren. So she decided to walk to where the headland jutted out and the columns of the ancient ruin showed golden against the grape blue of the darkening sea. She sat on a fallen block of sun-warmed marble trying to marshal her thoughts. She had only been here a few hours, but in that time she had learned that Colin was capable of having an affair with his Greek servant and that he had obviously attracted the attention of the young girl, Alex-andra. And where did she herself fit into the pic-ture?

She was puzzled and hurt. But she must give Colin time. Perhaps the situation was not to be seen in the vivid blacks and whites with which she saw it. So her mind seesawed from one thing to another and when she became aware that someone else had climbed the hill to the temple, she was almost relieved to have an inter-ruption to her thoughts.

Stavros stood before her, his face grave but not as totally disapproving as it had been at the cottage.

'Do you mind if I talk to you, Miss Grant?'

'It depends what you wish to talk about, Mr. De-metrios.'

He sat beside her on a marble block a little lower than her own. The sun of the late afternoon touched his classic features with a ruddy gold and made his ex-pression appear softer than hitherto.

'First, do you think we could dispense with formal-ities? We are to know each other for a little while and you are staying in my house. Could we use first names to each other? If I may call you Stacey then you can perhaps bring yourself to say "Stavros".'

He seemed to be making a genuine effort to be friendly and she nodded her consent, though she wondered whether she really could bring herself to address by his first name her rather cold and rigid host.

'Have you known Colin a long time?' he asked.

'Not very long.' And she explained how she had met him through Lauren, his sister, with whom she shared a flat.

'And you have developed some interest in him?'

Stacey felt herself blushing.

'I really don't see why I should answer that question.'

'You may think it strange, Miss Stacey, but since you are to be a guest in my house I cannot help but feel some responsibility for your welfare. Colin is a charming young man. Lately my young relative, Alexandra, has been showing a little too much interest in him. I cannot approve of this, since I have other plans for her. Greeks, you may know, have stricter ideas about a young girl's behaviour than is customary in Britain. I do not think that you should go alone to Colin's house without a proper chaperon. Obviously he is not to be trusted with young women.'

Although Stacey had been reaching the same conclusion herself during the course of this day, she was nettled with Stavros for stating this so clearly.

'You needn't worry about me, Mr ... Stavros. In England girls of my age are quite accustomed to looking after themselves.'

'But can they? That is the question. What chance has

a young girl of defending her honour with a man like Colin who has great charm and experience?'

'If you must know,' said Stacey, now thoroughly nettled by the reference to defending her honour, 'Colin spoke to me of marriage in London. I had every hope that he would still feel the same towards me here. His purpose in coming here was to write a book to increase his income in order to enable us to go on with this plan.'

'So,' said Stavros. 'That is interesting. But if it is so then can you tell me why he is paying attention to Alexandra and why the father of Chrysoula came to me to complain that Colin is ruining her chances with men of her own kind?'

Stacey was at a loss for words. She felt she hated Stavros for saying all these things against Colin.

'He probably regards Alexandra as a child – and as for Chrysoula, it seems to me that it's she who calls the tune.'

Stavros rose to his feet.

'Well, we shall see,' he said. 'I hope your faith in Colin is justified. But I still warn you to be careful and to give some regard to what I have said.'

The sun was setting now over the wine-dark sea. Stacey looked up at her companion. Silhouetted against the light, there was something menacing about the tall figure. How was it that in spite of his interest in her welfare she had this small frisson of alarm whenever she was in his company for very long? She felt that he was the one of whom she should be warned. Not Colin.

CHAPTER FIVE

IN the few days they had been here, a pattern seemed to have become established of bathing in the morning, sleeping in the afternoon and bathing again or making some expedition when it had become a little cooler. Stacey woke in the white-painted room that was simply furnished with bright-woven curtains and rugs. She opened her eyes to face another day that she knew she should have been enjoying. But the truth was that she felt the odd one in the gay company of Lauren, who usually paired off with Niko, and of Colin and Alexandra. Colin seemed to have been permitted time off from his work, but he certainly did not try to seek out her company. Try as she would to excuse him, in her heart she knew his promises had meant nothing. He was deeply involved now in his life on the island and there seemed no part in it for her.

There was a knock at the door and she called 'Come in!' preparing herself to say 'Kalimera' or 'Good morning' to the young maid who usually brought her the Continental breakfast of hot croissants, honey and coffee, but this morning she was greeted by a rather surly voice. Astonished, she found that it was Chrysoula who stood there with her tray, then slammed it down upon the table as if she would have liked to drop it on to the floor.

'Why, Chrysoula,' asked Stacey, 'what are you doing here?'

'I am working here,' said Chrysoula sharply. 'What

else? Since Kyrios Colin has decided he no longer requires me and since my father, the old devil, will not have me at home, Kyrios Demetrios has said I must come here to do extra work while they have visitors. Madam says if you have any washing to be done I must take it. Just leave it out, and when I have time I may do it.'

Having given this command in a cross tone of voice, she flounced out and banged the door. Stacey reflected that this kind of behaviour must be reserved for herself. She was sure Sophia would never tolerate it. She did not relish being at closer quarters with this girl who obviously regarded Colin as her property.

Lauren wandered in from the adjoining room. She was wearing a negligée that looked like a drift of seafoam and her dark red hair was hanging below her shoulders. How lovely she was, thought Stacey. No wonder Niko seemed to have eyes for no one else.

Lauren yawned and poured herself some coffee from the tray, buttering a croissant and roaming around the room dropping crumbs upon the red and white tiles.

'It's a heavenly day for sunbathing again,' she said. 'How lucky we are to have this glorious weather so early in the season. Niko said we could try another beach today. It's a pity that we always have to take the child Alexandra along. I find her a bit tiresome, but I can see that it might be advantageous to my darling brother in the long run. He doesn't seem to be making much progress with writing, so a wealthy young girl would be a fine solution to his problems.'

'Yes, I suppose so,' said Stacey.

'What's the matter, honey, you look a bit mopey? I had a small feeling that you entertained some hopes of

Colin yourself at one time. But, darling, I could have told you it wasn't any use. You can't pin him down, only if it's to his own advantage. You aren't really still pining for him, are you?'

'You needn't worry about me, Lauren,' said Stacey.

It was true she had come to terms with herself in the last day or so and had faced the fact that Colin had not cared for her as he had led her to believe. And she had not known the real Colin either. She had been too young and inexperienced about men to realize his character for what it was. She was disappointed, a bit humiliated perhaps, but, she hoped, heartwhole. Yet she found the whole situation embarrassing. She would be glad when the holiday was over, in spite of the loveliness of the island and Sophia's kindness.

'Had you forgotten, Lauren,' she reminded her friend, eager to change the subject, 'that we'd promised Sophia to go with her to the pottery and weaving school today?'

'Oh, good grief, Stacey, we can't waste a glorious morning looking at a stupid school!' Lauren protested, pulling a face.

'But she is our hostess and she's been awfully kind. I don't see how we can get out of it,' said Stacey. 'I think we would find it interesting.'

'You might,' said Lauren. 'I tell you what, Stacey. You can go with Sophia. I can say I made this arrangement with Niko before I knew about the other one.'

'Are you interested in Niko?' Stacey ventured to ask.

'He's a charmer, but another Colin, I think. The one

79

I would like to know better is Stavros. But he's too aloof. I think if you penetrated that cool dignity, you could find him very exciting. Don't you agree?'

'No, I don't really,' said Stacey. 'I think he's terribly difficult and cold as ice. He seems to disapprove of everything.'

'Don't be misled by that coldness. There's a suggestion of considerable charm. The trouble is one must find the key to unlock it. Given time I'm sure I could, and it would be most worthwhile, I can tell you.'

She could too, thought Stacey, looking at the laughing beauty of her heart-shaped face, the perfect lines of her body beneath the filmy negligée. Given the opportunity, Lauren could charm any man, even an unbending character like Stavros.

It was the custom in this house to breakfast in one's own room and the whole household did not assemble together until just before lunch. Stacey stayed in her room until she heard the others going off riding their donkeys to the beach. She listened a little enviously as she heard the gay laughter of the group and saw the girls in their gay towelling jackets that covered their swimsuits. Then she showered and putting on a pale green linen dress, she wound her hair around her head so that it would be cooler when she and Sophia walked to the school.

Sophia, in a dark-blue linen dress and a large straw hat, accepted Stacey's explanation for Lauren's absence with the utmost courtesy. She was a plump, gentle, dignified person, and Stacey wondered what had happened to her husband and what relation she bore to the two brothers.

'Are you taking Stacey to see the windmill first?'

asked Sox, who had suddenly appeared and was hopping along the path. 'Because if you are going there I will come too. The miller may let me work it. He did last time. But after that I am going fishing. I will leave Flavia behind.'

'Would you like to see the windmill?' asked Sophia. 'There are not a whole lot like the ones at Mykonos. Only a couple that have been kept for visitors to see.'

Twelve small pointed sails circled slowly in the light wind and the building was as dazzling white as the cottages. Inside it was just as white, and gently curved where the angles had been softened by layered whitewash. The wooden machinery made a noise creaking like a yacht in full sail and there was flour dust everywhere, although Sophia said the mill was not put to much practical use any more.

The miller let Sox work the mechanism with his assistance. The top was moveable and the whole upper works, thatched roof and sail wheel was able to revolve in order to catch the wind from any direction. After this Sox was satisfied and rejected the idea of coming to the weaving school.

'I have to go fishing with Dimitraki,' he declared.

'Have you tied Flavia up?' asked Sophia. 'She has a dreadful appetite for things she should not have.'

They watched him running, fleetfooted as the goat Flavia, down the path, turning to wave his whole face alight with puckish laughter before he disappeared from sight.

'You must be pleased you have such an intelligent, lively son,' Stacey commented.

Sophia smiled, a little astonished.

'But, my dear, didn't you know? He is not my son. He

81

is the son of Stavros. His mother was killed in a car accident when Socrates was a baby. Stavros was driving. It was a great tragedy for us all.'

So this perhaps explained why Stavros was more serious than his brother. If he had suffered such a tragedy quite early in his life, it was no wonder that he appeared aloof.

'Stavros is a cousin of mine. I was married to a man much older than myself and he died in the same year that Stavros lost Maria. It seemed suitable that I should come and keep house for him. He has been very good to me. And of course he is very fond of Alexandra.'

They had arrived at a building that looked a little larger than the rest. After the heat of the walk in the sun, the room into which they stepped seemed dark and cool. But the dim light held brilliant colour in the shape of rolls of cloth and different coloured hanks of yarn piled up on tables and shelves. A wooden loom stood beside the small window and a girl was working on it. It had a flat bed on an upright frame and the girl worked the pedals by foot but tossed the shuttle between the warp threads by hand. The material she was weaving was taking shape in varied stripes of subtle colours, misty blues and greens and purples like the bloom on a grape.

There were other weavers in the inside rooms and another room where a dark-haired man was working a potter's wheel while young girls painted terra-cotta bowls with sure swift strokes in classic designs.

'The islands are all very poor,' Sophia explained. 'Stavros likes to encourage them to help themselves by making such things for the tourist trade. They are sent to shops in Athens. If it had not been for his help the island would have died long ago.'

Stacey found that her idea of Stavros as a wealthy business tycoon who was not really interested in ordinary people was forced to change.

'And now,' said Sophia, 'you would like to take a drink in the office of Stavros, yes?'

Stacey was confused. 'But won't we disturb his work?' she asked.

'His work is holiday to him here. He looks after vines and so on for recreation. He will be glad to be interrupted by us, especially by one of his charming visitors.'

'Well, you know best, Sophia,' said Stacey. But inwardly she wondered whether he would be pleased to see her, since every time they met she seemed to face his disapproval.

Sophia led the way to another white building and here there were archways, the high vaulting making the place cool. There were vats of wine too, but not much sign of activity, for the workers were all out on the upper slopes caring for the young vines.

However, they found Stavros talking to his manager in a simple office with a roll-top desk. He welcomed them with smiling courtesy and Stacey reflected that he seemed very fond of Sophia, for he showed towards her more affection than she had thought it possible when she had first met him.

He asked the manager to bring a bottle of wine and they sat in the sun on the patio at the back of the building. Beyond this the slopes of the hillside were covered with the regular pattern of young green vines, and the pale leaves seemed to have a luminous quality of their own. The golden wine was light and refreshing and the sun was warm but not hot. For the first time in the last few days, Stacey found she had forgotten her worries about Colin and could begin to enjoy the sense of well-being that life on the island seemed to bring.

'And where are the others?' asked Stavros.

'How can you ask? They are bathing or sunbathing as usual,' Sophia said. 'Stacey is the one who is kind enough to consent to be bored with my interests. But now, Stavros, you can reward her for this great courtesy with an older woman. I thought perhaps you could take her for a sail.'

Stacey was embarrassed by Sophia's well-meaning efforts to give her some entertainment. She was sure that to take her sailing was the last thing that Stavros wanted to do. But whatever his feelings were, he responded with the good manners of a host.

'That would give me pleasure. Would you like to go sailing?'

'There is nothing more delightful on the Aegean. The day is perfect for such a thing,' Sophia assured her, smiling.

'Will you come too?' asked Stacey.

'No, my child. My sailing days are over, except on the larger yacht where I can be a passenger. But I assure you that Stavros is to be trusted on the sea. He is a very good yachtsman.'

Again it seemed she was to be thrust into his company, not knowing whether he was pleased about this but suspecting otherwise.

The harbour was the deep green of a tourmaline and the sea was shot with sapphire and emerald. The small keeler with its yellow hull looked trim and neat, bobbing in the water beside the jetty.

'You will find some of Alexandra's slacks in the cabin,' Sophia had told her, and she changed into the tight narrow navy trousers and the red and white striped top while Stavros was fixing up the sails. Stavros wore only a pair of yellow shorts that seemed to emphasize his deep golden tan.

He seemed immensely at home in a boat and she followed his instructions easily as they sped over the calm waters of the harbour towards the more turbulent waves of the outer sea. It was a heavenly day for sailing. The boat climbed over the long lazy swells of the crystal green waves with effortless grace. Stacey forgot her nervousness and began to enjoy the feeling of being borne along as if on the back of a great white-winged bird.

Stavros smiled to see her pleasure. He seemed now to her utterly different from the rather gloomy man she had imagined he was when she first met him. His smile was gay and attractive and she could not help laughing back at him when they were showered with spray or bounced over the waves.

'Do you like it?' he asked, raising his voice above the noise of the windblown sails.

'It's the most heavenly sensation,' she answered. 'I feel like a dolphin.'

'Well, there are some of your companions,' he rejoined, and there, diving along in the wake of the boat, she saw about five of these large graceful creatures playing and gambolling as if they too loved the movement of the waves and wind. She had forgotten her first feeling that he was taking her on this trip because he had been forced to do so by Sophia. Seeing him at the helm, so relaxed, so carefree, she felt that this was what he really wanted to do and that it did not matter whose company he had, so long as that person obeyed his commands.

Reaching back, the breeze died a little and he decided they should put up the spinnaker to catch more of the wind. Like everything else on the boat it was in perfect order and it sped up effortlessly, ballooning out in a glorious coloured dome of striped yellow and flame colour. Up and down over the gentle swells they sped until Stacey felt they might have been flying, so effortlessly they raced along. She watched Stavros carefully as he held the tiller and he smiled back at her; for once it seemed utterly free of the dark thoughts that seemed to plague him in his normal life.

She felt she was getting a glimpse of the man Stavros must have been when he was young and free of care as Niko was now. They were approaching a small bay on the other side of the island and took in some sail.

'Would you care to have lunch?' he asked. 'We can anchor here and go ashore across the rocks. There's a small *taverna* where we can get seafood. It won't be like the Ritz, for example, but the food will be quite eatable.'

How pleasant he could be, thought Stacey. After the emotions and disappointments of the last few days, it was good to feel enjoyment again in the simple pleasures of sailing and even in the anticipation of eating lunch with this man who had before seemed so unapproachable but was now a charming companion. As she combed her hair and washed in the rather primitive cloakroom, she felt she had dispensed with all regrets for Colin's careless neglect, and she came out looking forward eagerly to her meal and to the homeward sail.

'Come and choose your lunch,' said Stavros, taking her arm and leading her to a tank where live lobsters swam. He laughed at her distressed expression and assured her that crustaceans really felt no pain.

'I feel terrible because I'm enjoying the poor thing so much,' she confessed some time later as she forked out the tender white meat from its shell.

They lingered over coffee and she confessed that at last she was getting used to the bitter brew. The time had sped by as swiftly as their boat had sailed over the blue Aegean. It was amazing, she thought. During the whole afternoon she had never been at a loss for words with him, and yet before he had made her feel awkward and shy. She felt a heightened awareness of him that she had never experienced before and thought that she must have imagined that cold sneer, for now his smile was warm and gay.

He asked her about her life and work in London.

'Do you intend to remain with this firm?' he said when she had told him what humble work she did at the dressmaking establishment where Lauren modelled.

'I'm not certain whether the job will still be open for me when we return. It was because of Lauren that I had the opportunity to come here, but the job itself was temporary and I think I may have to look for another one when I get back.'

'I suppose it depends upon your friend Colin's plans too,' he said. She was confused by this, but did not know how to deny it. Before she had decided what to say, he continued, 'I think I should tell you that I took it upon myself to inform Alexandra of the true situation between yourself and Colin.'

Stacey's feeling of carefree gaiety vanished. If he had thrown the cup of coffee in her face she could not have been more shocked.

'But ... but what did you say to her?' she stammered.

'I told her that you gave me to understand that you considered yourself affianced to Colin. I thought that if she knew this she would not consider Colin as a possible suitor. I am afraid that was the way her thoughts were tending, and certainly, as I told you before, I have others plans for her.'

Sophia had said he himself was very fond of Alexandra. Could that be his plan? But how terrible that he had given Alexandra the impression that she herself was engaged to Colin when really nothing could be further from the truth. How she wished she had never spoken of it to Stavros. Of course he had taken it very seriously because that is how the Greeks did think about these things. And she had been serious at the time. But she should never have said she considered herself engaged to Colin.

Perhaps it had been so in London. But now London seemed a million miles away and the young Stacey who had been so thrilled with her first acquaintance with a sophisticated city man seemed a different person from the one she had become in these few short days on the Greek island, a person a little sadder, a little more grown-up and certainly wiser. What could she do to right the impression that Stavros had?

'You're mistaken. We are not formally engaged,' she assured him.

The dark eyes regarded her quizzically, almost tenderly.

'My dear Stacey, at the moment you feel like this because your feelings have been hurt. But I believe you will come back to Colin. Lovers' quarrels are soon

88

over.'

'I thought you disapproved of Colin?'

'With regard to Alexandra, yes, I do disapprove, but I have no right, I realize, to interfere with your plans. When I spoke to you before I was trying to protect you as a guest in my house. But when you told me you were betrothed to him it put a different complexion on the matter.'

'But I'm not certain now . . .' Stacey began, very conscious that she was becoming more and more entangled in this misunderstanding.

His dark eyes regarded her very seriously. The laughing companion of the afternoon's sail had vanished.

'Even if you feel uncertain, I would be grateful if you could let Alexandra continue to believe in this betrothal. It would be better that way for all concerned.'

She felt unable to argue about it any further. It was best to leave it and await events. But she could not help hoping that she could persuade Lauren to leave as soon as possible.

CHAPTER SIX

LAMBRINI, the little brown donkey, brought Stacey up the hill to the house, for Stavros had stayed behind to clear up a little work at his office. She was looking forward to having a bath and changing for dinner. The sail had been lovely, but her hair and face were covered with the fine salt deposit of the sea spray. Tonight she had made up her mind that she would shake off all depressing thoughts and dress up to try to look really glamorous. At least that would do her morale good even if it did not impress anyone else.

She thought over what she should wear from her small wardrobe of clothes and decided upon a kaftan of pure silk in shades of turquoise and lilac. It was a terrace dress, full length and long-sleeved, and was one to make her feel more dignified and confident, the only truly beautiful dress she possessed. As she brushed the curly tendrils of her newly-washed hair and applied a light make-up over her skin she noticed that the day in the sun had enhanced her looks. For the first time since she had come here she felt she looked attractive. There was a luminous glow to her brown eyes and a peachlike radiance to her sun-touched skin.

When she joined the others in the courtyard for aperitifs it was evident that she had not been mistaken. Niko gave a frank whistle of admiration and she noticed that Colin frowned at this.

'How lovely you look, my dear,' said Sophia. 'Don't you agree, Stavros? Your sailing expedition must have been good for Stacey.'

Stavros was standing in the darkness beyond the pool of light cast by the terrace lamps, but now he came forward and at Sophia's command took a good look at Stacey. In his dark formal suit with the white linen shirt, he looked very different from the gay yachtsman of the afternoon. Although she was conscious that she was looking more lovely than usual, she felt embarrassed by the gaze of those dark eyes that were concentrated upon her. She turned aside in confusion and accepted the drink that Niko offered to her, taking a mouthful without even knowing what she was tasting. Why, in spite of the friendlier atmosphere of the day's sailing, could he always have this effect on her? Even when she had tried to look pleasing, he still seemed to look at her as if there were something about her of which he disapproved.

Now Colin was at her side and whispering only for her. How well she remembered how he could make you feel cherished by murmuring in a crowd something that was intended only for your ears.

'How exquisite you look, my Stacey. Do you remember when we chose that dress together?'

Yes, she remembered. He had taken her to a boutique that sold Indian garments and she had paid far more for it than she could really afford because Colin had said the dress was made for her. But she was no longer his Stacey. She must remember that and not be led away any longer by his insidious charm.

'Where's Alexandra?' she asked.

He smiled. 'My downright Stacey! What does it matter? The poor child has had a little too much sun. She's had a tray sent up to her room. But don't worry about her. She can't hold a candle to you tonight.'

Lauren had crossed over to Stavros and had engaged him in conversation. It was not unusual for her to look lovely, of course. Tonight she was wearing a dress in colours of peacock blue and emerald and her deep-copper hair was piled high above her small head. Long golden ear-rings swung from her ears and the bodice of the dress, tied in halter fashion at her neck, revealed her golden perfect back. How did she make Stavros smile so easily? Stacey wondered. She would like to have known what his wife had looked like, for he obviously admired beauty in women.

'You aren't paying enough attention to me,' Colin complained. 'What has Stavros got to deserve that concentrated gaze from those beautiful brown eyes? They're mine, remember, and they should be looking at me.'

She looked at him, puzzled by his sudden change of attitude. How could he suddenly start to pay her attention when for the whole time they had been here he had seemed to try to avoid her? There was no understanding him, she thought. And she was not at all sure that she wanted to. For her his charm had gone. It had begun to vanish when she had seen Chrysoula in his arms and again when he had hurt her by showing how interested he was in Alexandra.

After dinner, Lauren persuaded the company to dance to records. It was better, she declared, then the Greek custom of the men dancing on their own. She waltzed into the arms of her host and Stavros had no choice but to follow her lead. But he did not look unwilling. He was a good dancer, light and graceful. Together he and Lauren made a very distinguished couple with their tall good looks. Niko had persuaded

Sophia to dance, for he evidently did not want to disturb Stacey and Colin, but now Colin sprang up, leaving for the moment the whispered intimacies with which he was entertaining her.

'Come, my love,' he said, and now she was in his arms. If this had happened the first night of their arrival, she would have been delighted and joyous, but it was too late now. She realized that Colin was only making a fuss of her this evening because she looked more than usually attractive and because Alexandra was absent.

She noticed that Stavros was looking at them rather speculatively and thought that now he would believe he was right in telling Alexandra that she and Colin intended to marry. Well, if it had the result he wished for, that was, to frighten Alexandra off, she would not mind. If only she could get away from the island ... and quickly too. She must say to Lauren that she would like to go, and yet looking at Lauren laughing up into the face of her host she thought it would be difficult to get her to cut her visit short.

'The moon is full tonight. You must see the view of the citadel from the front terrace,' Colin insisted, and he drew her away before she could protest, through the hall and out of the front door to stand on the terraced balustrade above the sweeping marble steps.

A path of moonlight shone silver across the sea and above them on the headland the broken columns of the citadel were dark against the deep blue of the sky. In the still night sounds travelled clearly, the bleat of a kid, the plaintive call of a little donkey wanting its companions.

'It's heavenly,' said Stacey, forgetting about Colin for

the moment and concentrating on the beauty of the scene.

'So you understand now why I've stayed here?' said Colin. He put his arm around her and turned her to face him. 'Dearest little Stacey, you're so sweet. Why have you been avoiding me?'

She was taken aback and did not know how to reply to him. But he did not seem to require an answer, for he took her in his arms and pressed his lips upon hers.

'I've been waiting for this,' he said. 'I'd forgotten what a fascinating thing you are, Stacey.'

She draw away from him, for she was sure that it was only the moonlight and her attractive appearance to-night that had caused Colin to pay her more attention. At the same moment there was a sound, as if someone had moved in the deep shade cast by one of the pillars.

'What was that?' asked Stacey.

'You're trying to distract me,' Colin accused her. 'I remember how delightfully shy you always were. It was nothing, only a kid moving on the hillside.'

'I think we'd better go in, Colin. The others will be missing us.'

'Not Lauren and Stavros. If I know my sister she intends to set her cap at that man, and I don't blame her. What a catch he would be! But come, Stacey. You weren't as cold as this in London. Remember?'

He embraced her again and as he did so she was aware of a movement behind them. Lauren and Stavros had come out on to the terrace too and Lauren, seeing them, laughed on a tinkling silvery note.

'My dear brother doesn't waste any time, does he? What are you two doing out here? Admiring the view, I

94

suppose.'

Stacey felt confused and miserable. She wished Stavros had not seen her with Colin. It would only confirm his opinion that she was deeply involved with him. But why should that matter? In her own mind she had surprised a strange thought, the desire that it had been Stavros with whom she had admired the moonlit sea and not Colin.

Sophia came out fanning herself. 'I am not used to such gaiety,' she protested. 'Stavros, you should dance with both of your young guests – I am sure Niko is dying to dance with Lauren now. I will go to fetch more coffee from the kitchen. The servants will have gone by now. Will you come and help me, Colin?'

He had no alternative but to go with Sophia, and Stavros turned to Stacey as Niko whirled Lauren back to help choose another record.

'Would you like to dance, Stacey? We can hear the music from here.'

To her surprise he put his arms around her there on the moonlit terrace and began to dance to the sound of the music. Lauren had chosen a quiet romantic tune and Stacey found herself moving slowly, becoming more and more deeply aware of the man whose half-smiling mouth was in such close proximity to hers. She was bewildered by the rush of deep emotion she felt and tried to tell herself sternly that the moonlit night, the silvery scene and the romantic music were a heady mixture. But she had not felt like this with Colin. Quite the contrary. She yielded to the temptation and forgetting thoughts of common sense, she gave herself up to the beauty of this perfect night and the thrilling sensations that she felt while dancing with this man whom she had hitherto regarded as cold.

The music came to an end and they could hear Sophia's voice calling them in for coffee. The dancing was over and yet she was still in his arms and he was regarding her with an expression she could not read.

'I apologize, Stacey – for the moment I had forgotten. You must go back to Colin. I have kept you here too long.'

She wanted to deny this, to tell him that Colin meant nothing to her any more, but she was afraid that her voice would betray the depth of the feelings she had just experienced. Wordlessly she followed him to join the others, but then, pleading tiredness, she excused herself and went up to her room. She wanted to be alone to think over the thrilling emotions she had felt during the last half hour, but when she opened the door into her apartment she was immediately aware that there was someone there in the moonlit room.

'Don't put on the light,' said a voice. 'I would rather speak to you without it.'

'Alexandra! I thought you were ill. What are you doing here, child? You should be in bed.'

'I'm not a child to be sent to bed, although my mother seems to think so.'

Contrary to her wishes, Stacey had turned on the lamp at her bedside and in the soft golden light she could see the girl's dark eyes, dilated and distressed.

'Stavros told me today that you are engaged to Colin. But it can't be true. Colin intends to marry me. He has said so.'

Now Stacey felt herself to be in a dilemma. She had half promised Stavros she would let Alexandra believe that she intended to marry Colin. Indeed, Stavros appeared to believe this himself, in spite of her denials.

'We've never been formally engaged,' she said.

'That makes no difference, don't you see? If Colin has promised to marry you, Stavros would never let him marry me. He is so strict about these things. I could never get his consent if he thought I had taken Colin from his fiancée.'

'But you're very young, Alexandra. Colin may not be the one for you. You'll probably meet many men before you decide to marry one finally.'

Alexandra shrugged her shoulders and pouted with a childish expression. Her face was bare of make-up. She was clad only in filmy yellow pyjamas with a transparent jacket and she looked about fourteen yet deliciously enchanting.

'I have decided to marry Colin, and I can tell you this – that as far as he is concerned you haven't a hope. It is me he loves and I will fight to keep him. I am not such a child as you all seem to think!'

Stacey wanted to tell her she was no longer interested in Colin, but she knew that Stavros would not want this.

'What about your mother? What does Sophia think of this?'

Alexandra threw out her hands in a gesture of despair.

'What do you think? My mother has always hoped I would marry Stavros. I know this. Can you imagine it? He is rich, yes. But he is too old and strict for me.'

'And Stavros? How does he feel?'

'Oh, I expect he would marry me if I wanted it. He has not cared for any woman since Maria died.'

She threw aside the idea of marriage to Stavros with

the carelessness of a young girl who has never really experienced any deep feeling, thought Stacey. But why should she herself feel so hurt by this conversation?

'Promise me,' demanded Alexandra, 'that you will not stand in my way where Colin is concerned. But even if you do, it will be no use. I intend to have him.'

'I can't promise you anything,' said Stacey, thinking of her conversation with Stavros.

Alexandra was like a spoiled child who has always had everything, and now she was demanding to have Colin. But now that Stacey knew more of him she wondered whether he was the one for Alexandra. She could not blame Stavros for objecting to her infatuation. But did he intend to marry the young girl himself? She remembered how carefully he had chosen the present of the necklace on Rhodes. It must be true that he was very fond of her.

The next morning when Lauren came in to share her breakfast tray, Stacey screwed up her courage to state what had been in her mind for the last day or so.

'Lauren, how long are you intending to stay here? Don't you think we'd better think of going home soon?'

'Home? Are you mad? We've only just settled down. Why on earth should we leave? It's beautifully comfortable here. And we'll never get such a chance again. Imagine staying in this lovely house on a Greek island! Most people would give their souls to be having this experience. Really, Stacey, just because Colin is more interested in Alexandra at the moment – and I really can't blame him for that – there's no need for you to try to spoil our holiday. I think it's fabulous, and last night for the first time I seemed to get Stavros a little interested. Surely you can't be so selfish as to want to go now?'

Perhaps she was being selfish, Stacey reflected. She could not fully understand herself the fact that she desired above all else to get away from Paxados. She felt as if she were on the brink of a dangerous whirlpool. And this had nothing to do with the feeling she had had for Colin. Somehow now the emotion she had felt for Colin in London seemed that of a very young girl playing at being in love. Why now did she feel that she must escape before she experienced the deeper, more dangerous emotions of a woman?

CHAPTER SEVEN

CHRYSOULA burst into the room without knocking and stood there watching Stacey as she hastily put on her dressing gown over her brief underwear. The dark, tempestuous girl looked the other up and down as if comparing Stacey's slim figure with her own riper charms.

'You enjoy yourself last night, yes?' she said in a familiar tone.

'What do you mean, Chrysoula?' asked Stacey.

She had grown to dread an encounter with the fiery Chrysoula, for she saw a kind of hatred in the other girl's eyes and there was nothing she could do to appease her. She knew, of course, it was all to do with Colin.

'I saw you first with Colin, then with Kyrios Stavros upon the balcony.' She laughed scornfully. 'Two men in one evening! And I thought Englishwomen were cold. But Colin cares nothing for you, he told me so. And the other one? What a hope!'

Stacey thought it best to ignore the girl. She would not become involved in an argument with her. She eyed the little pile of clothing that Chrysoula carried and said, 'Is that our laundry? Thank you so much, Chrysoula. We're grateful that you did it for us.'

There was a wicked glint in the girl's eyes.

'You may not be so pleased when you see it. The little one's goat has been at it. How unfortunate! Sad to tell, some of your clothes are beyond mending.'

She flung the clothing on the bed and went out, banging the door behind her. When Stacey examined the clothes they were indeed in a sorry state. They were all hers, not Lauren's. She strongly suspected Chrysoula and allowed this to happen on purpose, for everyone knew that Flavia had a propensity for chewing anything she came across. The clothing that had been washed was usually put well out of her reach. Having come by air, Stacey had not a great deal of luggage with her and she could ill afford to lose any clothing. She decided she could not tell Sophia about it after all her kindness.

But it was not to be as easy as that. Before she could put the clothing away there was a knock at the door and Sophia herself stood there.

'My dear, I am sorry to interrupt you so early, but Stavros asked me to call while you were still here. He thought perhaps you had plans for a swim and wants to see you before you go out. He is in his study.' Her eyes fell upon the ruined clothes. 'But, my dear child, what has happened here?'

'Oh, Sophia, I didn't mean you to see them. It doesn't matter at all. Chrysoula washed them and unfortunately Flavia chewed them.'

'Oh, that girl! She is unbelievable. If it wasn't that Stavros had promised her father that she could work here, I would never have engaged her. We must replace them. But how? There are no suitable clothes on the island. We must plan something.'

'Please, Sophia, don't worry about it. Why does Stavros want to see me?'

The matter of the clothes seemed secondary. From the moment Sophia had mentioned Stavros, Stacey's heart had started to beat faster and her legs felt weak.

How stupid she was, she thought, and pondered the necessity of departure while the less sensible side of her mind was thrilled at the idea of meeting Stavros this morning. She dressed in a tawny material that fortunately had escaped Flavia's attention. As she brushed her hair she noticed that her hands were trembling and the silky tendrils escaped from the style that she had hoped to make neat.

When she was ready she rang the bell as Sophia had instructed and a manservant came to show her where to go. Their time had been spent for the most part living out of doors in the courtyard and in their own rooms and Stacey was not familiar with the layout of the rest of the house. It appeared that Stavros had his own suite of rooms which included the austere whitewashed room in which she now found herself. Bookshelves lined one wall and she observed a simply designed record player and radio. The chairs were of dark red leather and the curtains of heavy woven cloth. She looked around for photographs, but there were none, and the pictures were modern yet austere, telling her no more of this man's personality than she already knew.

From the window there was a view of the ruined columns, golden now in the morning light and thronged with swooping birds, flashing blue in their swift flight, with a background of sea the colour of tourmaline.

He came in quietly, and yet she was aware of him the moment he entered the room. She turned reluctantly, for she was afraid she would betray the excitement she felt at his approach, the strange mixture of fear and joy. This morning she had felt like a child, a young school-girl summoned to see the principal, and had even wondered whether she had unwittingly done something which merited criticism, so sure she was that he always disapproved of her behaviour. But now when she saw his smile she experienced a feeling of relief.

'Thank you for giving me your time, Stacey. I know you must be eager to make the most of your holiday and they tell me Colin is keen on these swimming expeditions.'

It was no use, she thought, trying to tell him that she was no longer concerned with Colin's interests. He would not believe her. She glanced at him and found it hard to read his expression, for the classical features always seemed to wear a restrained look as if their owner did not want to show his feelings to the world at large. She wondered whether he had always looked like that or if the tragedy of his wife's death had affected him so much that his natural gaiety had disappeared. For on occasion she had seen him laugh naturally and freely, but this had not happened very often in their acquaintance.

'Stacey, since you tell me that you have no settled work to go back to in London, I was wondering whether you would consider staying a while longer. My son, Socrates, seems to like you and I'm afraid during the summer his education is usually sadly neglected. I wondered whether if you stayed a while with us you would consider giving him some informal instruction in English.'

'But I thought Colin was responsible for that.'

Stavros smiled a little wryly.

'That was the idea, yes. But I'm afraid Colin's duties in the library have superseded my son's education. He tells me he does not have time to give much attention to teaching Socrates.'

This was absurd, Stacey well knew. Colin had plenty of time to spend with Alexandra. No wonder Stavros smiled so cynically!

'Sophia has been very kind. I would willingly repay your hospitality by talking English to Socrates, but . . .'

Stavros interrupted her with a wave of his hand. His dark eyes flashed as he shook his head.

'That is not the question. As I said before, you have a strange idea of Greek hospitality if you think you must repay us for what is the natural thing to do. No, Stacey. If you taught Socrates of course I would expect you to accept payment for it. But I'm sorry I interrupted you. What did you intend to say?'

'I was going to say that I've enjoyed this stay on the island, of course. You've been most kind to entertain strangers. But I hope to leave in a few days' time. In fact I was thinking of going back to London as soon as possible.'

A blank look veiled the effect of this statement upon Stavros, but in the first moment she had detected an emotion that seemed half anger, half some other one . . . could it be indignant pride?

'So,' he said, his dark eyes smouldering, 'you are not happy on Paxados?'

She lifted her eyes to meet his. She too, she felt, could be allowed a little pride.

'To be honest,' she admitted, 'I've found myself in a difficult position here.'

'You mean that your fiancé had become interested in other women while you were apart? But, Stacey, you do not know men. You should realize that most men behave like this when the women to whom they are pledged are far away.'

'That's not what you told me when we first spoke of this,' Stacey accused him. 'And if it is so, I don't want anything to do with men like this.'

He smiled a little bitterly.

'You have the intolerance of the very young. And what good do you think you will do in this situation by running back to London? Or do you think Colin will follow you?'

He was making her furious with his lack of perception.

'You don't understand,' she said. 'I just want to get away.'

'I understand one thing. You would be doing me a great favour if you would consent to stay here. I am anxious that Socrates should stop running wild as he has been doing of late, but most of all I wish that Alexandra should see sense, and she will only do so if she knows that Colin is pledged to you. I am sure that Colin's real interest lies with you. He has merely been diverted by circumstances. Does he realize, by the way, that if Alexandra marries without my consent and when she is under age she will not get one penny of the money her grandfather left to her? If you were to tell him that I think his interest in you would be quickly restored.'

'You're impossible!' Stacey cried. 'I can read your mind clearly. You want Colin to have his interest in me revived so that you can snatch Alexandra from any danger. And yet you insult my so-called fiancé by implying that he's only interested in her money. I will not stay here so that your own plans can be worked out without any disaster interrupting them!'

His eyes narrowed. She sensed the anger behind the

cool dark expression.

'So. Marriage to Colin for Alexandra would be a disaster. And yet it would be for you your heart's desire. Isn't that so?'

He was twisting her words just as he seemed to be able to twist her emotions.

'I know it's useless to deny to you that I'm in love with Colin, but I wish Alexandra no harm.'

'Then stay here,' he urged. 'If you stay, Alexandra will get over her infatuation. I will see to that.'

His mouth was determined and she thought she would not like to be the young Alexandra if she were trying to oppose him. But then what was she herself to do?

She turned and looked out of the window. The swallows were still making their joyous flight between the broken columns of marble that had faded to deep gold. He crossed the room silently and put his hands on her shoulders.

'Look,' he said. 'The swallows have only just returned. The whole summer is before them too. If you stay, Sophia will be so delighted. It is lonely for her here and she seems to enjoy your company. Soon we will begin to make expeditions to the other islands – Crete, Santorin. They are all within reach if we take the large yacht. And I am sure Colin will be delighted too. The reason for his flirtatious behaviour is because he has missed you. Say you will stay.'

But when she turned and nodded, not trusting herself to speak, it was not Colin she was thinking of. How could she think of anyone else when his hands were warm on her shoulders, his mouth transformed from anger and smiling so close to hers?

Sophia was delighted with this new decision that they should stay longer. Lauren had had a phone call from Athens from the firm for whom she had done fashion modelling to ask her to hold herself in readiness to do some more if it would fit in with her other assignments. This gave her the excuse she needed to put off her return to London, for Sophia declared it would be easy for her to fly to Athens with Stavros on one of his business trips.

Lauren seemed very happy so long as she could laze in the sun and acquire a glorious tan. Unusually for a person with her colour of hair, she had a creamy opaque skin which tanned to a beautiful gold and it was just what she needed for her photographic assignments. But Stacey was glad to find a little more to do. Her duties to Sox were light, but she tried to be conscientious in teaching him. The lessons were informal, to say the least. She accompanied him on walks talking English to him and, since he was as lively as a grasshopper, she had quite a task to keep up with him while trying to carry out the work of educating this lively little boy.

This morning they had come up to the citadel on the hill above the house, for it had become one of their favourite places for lessons. From here one could look down and view the whole island, the white circle of the village on the edge of the harbour, the groves of olive trees as the path ascended, and the plantations of vines. There was a scent of thyme and pine needles. Dragonflies darted through the air, their wings glittering, and cicadas reverberated their piercing sound from their hiding places. There were white goats grazing amongst the olive trees and Flavia, who usually accompanied them, greeted the sound of their plaintive bleatings with a more aggressive note of her own. She was growing by the day into a strong little animal, with hard head and small horns that could give a painful butt, hard little hooves and glittering wicked eyes that seemed to seek out mischief. If Stacey set down the books she was carrying she had to remember in case Flavia decided to make a meal of them.

But Sox thought the world of her. Dimitraki could not always play with him for, young as he was, his father required him to help in the fields, but Flavia was always there, a willing companion who could be talked to as she chewed the yellow flowers and looked, Sox assured her, pure and pretty as an angel.

'But she can be a wicked beast, I know,' Sox told Stacey. 'I heard Sophia telling Stavros how she ate your clothes and saying something must be done to replace them.'

Stacey felt embarrassed. She wished Sophia had not chosen to tell Stavros. He would think she had complained.

'But you know that was not really Flavia's fault. She cannot help being a goat and Chrysoula knew she would eat them if they were left around. It was Chrysoula's fault. She does not like you, Stacey. But I do, so you need not worry about her. I won't let her do you any more harm.'

He spoke so bravely that she had to repress a smile, for he was deadly serious. Nevertheless she was touched.

'You are a *pallikari*,' she assured him, having learned the word recently. He smiled and looked pleased. For this was high praise, meaning he was a brave young man.

108

'You learn Greek well, but not as good as my English,' he assured her.

At lunch time that day Lauren was very excited because she had received another call from Athens and they wanted to know whether she could go there for a day in order to model more clothes for an international fashion magazine.

'That all seems to fit in well,' said Sophia, nodding her approval. 'As soon as Stavros arrives we will confirm it, but I know certainly that he will be travelling to Athens very soon. You will be able to go with him and you can stay the night at our town house. It will all be quite *comme il faut*, for our Aunt Hélène who is eighty and does not care for Paxados stays there and she makes good chaperon together with our housekeeper. Even I am afraid of Cassandra.'

'Is that really her name?' asked Lauren. 'How devastating!'

'One finds the old Greek names over and over in modern Greece. Names like Sophocles, Pericles ... it is all part of our tradition.'

Then turning to Stacey, she said, 'And you, Stacey, you must go too. It will only be for a day, but it means I can replace those clothes for you. I still feel guilty for Chrysoula's sin, not to mention the wicked Flavia.'

'But, Sophia, there is no need whatsoever to do anything about it. I've forgotten about them already.'

'No, I insist. You must go too.'

'There's no necessity,' said Lauren hastily. Obviously she was not keen to have Stacey's company when there was the chance of travelling alone with Stavros. 'I can easily lend her clothes if she needs any more.'

This was the first Stacey had heard of such an offer,

and in any case Lauren was much taller than she.

'No, I would feel much better if Stacey bought some replacements in Athens. I cannot have you sacrificing your clothes when it is the fault of an employee of ours,' said Sophia firmly. 'Perhaps we can persuade Alexandra to go too. Would you like that, my darling?'

But Sophia's daughter was strangely silent. She, who was supposed to have such a passion for the city, said now that she was perfectly happy here and that Athens would be too hot, the journey too tiring.

'I will go, if Stavros agrees,' said Niko. 'It will be good to see Athens again even if all that interests one has departed.'

'You mean that all your girl-friends are on the French Riviera or at the Italian Lakes,' chaffed Alexandra.

'But it would be good to drive my car again,' Niko said. 'Lauren, I insist that you come for a drive with me as soon as you are free.'

'We'll see,' said Lauren, smiling enigmatically. It was obvious that she wanted to see whether Stavros was available first.

'Stacey, how about you? I know you will take pity on me. We will arrange to have lunch together when you have finished your shopping.'

When Stavros came in for his aperitif, everything had already been arranged and Stacey thought he could hardly have gone against Sophia's wishes, whatever he privately thought of it. But obviously he would not mind taking Lauren for a trip to Athens. She was such a lovely creature to show off in the night spots. No man could fail to be proud of being seen in her company. She herself could not help feeling a little *de trop*. But she would try to keep out of the way as much as possible. It was quite evident that Lauren had been reluctant that she should accompany them.

Sophia insisted that Stacey should go to the shops where she herself had an account. Stacey demurred, for she knew she could never afford the prices, but Sophia was adamant. She must be allowed to pay for a replacement of the clothes that Flavia and Chrysoula had destroyed between them.

CHAPTER EIGHT

IT seemed amazing after being in quiet Paxados to find themselves in the busy centre of Athens. In the private jet belonging to the Demetrios family, the journey had been very brief, and yet the city seemed a different world from the slow, other-worldly pace of the small island.

They had arrived early in the morning and Stavros had disappeared upon his business calls. Lauren, after making some phone calls, had been collected by taxi to be transported to the studios and Niko had gone about his own private affairs, but before he went he remembered his promise to take Stacey to lunch.

'Do you think you could find your way to the Royal Hellenic Yacht Club?' he asked, and left her with the address in her handbag carefully written in the Greek alphabet with instructions to the taxi driver in case he did not speak English.

All roads in Athens seemed to lead to Syntagma Square and Stacey found the small shops that Sophia recommended were near there too. She was delighted with the underwear and summer dresses shown to her by the eager saleswoman, but shocked as she calculated the price in drachmas back to pounds and pence. However, she had been given some idea of prices by Sophia, who was amused at her concern, so she knew her purchases were within the bounds she had been set. She bought a couple of sets of underwear, exquisitely hand-worked, and two dresses, one in pale blue linen and the other in a more dressy style of pure silk in a Pucci print. They were to be delivered at the town house, so she did not have to carry the parcel.

Having finished her shopping fairly early, she sat at a table in front of a café while she decided what to do next. It was very different from Paxados. The shop windows were full of the most elaborate-looking confections, sweets, cakes of every kind, together with crystallized fruits and Turkish delight of jewel-like colours. The streets and people, she decided, looked a little drab, not quite as lively as London. Perhaps this was because the women seemed to favour black as a universal colour for their clothes and the men also wore dark suits. But if their clothes lacked colour certainly their conversation seemed to make up for it. They talked so much at the tables around her that she wondered how they ever heard what the other said.

She was served with a cup of black coffee and a glass of water. Here was one thing that was the same as in Paxados. A vendor, immediately discerning that she was a foreigner, came to ask her to purchase the pistachio nuts he was selling. She bought some of the fascinating small nuts in their red open shells and found they were as delicious as he had told her. She sat for a long time watching the passing scene and drinking the coffee. No one disturbed her. As far as she could see, you were at liberty to sit here for a couple of hours if you wanted to.

But now she must try to find her way to Piraeus if she was to keep her appointment with Niko to have lunch with him. He had carelessly suggested that she should take a taxi, but he did not realize the limitations of her finances. She must find a less expensive way to get there.

She asked the waiter and he directed her to take a tram to Omonia Square where she could get the underground train and from there she would only have a short taxi drive to the Yacht Club. In the streets where she had spent the morning, in the vicinity of Syntagma Square, the shops had been luxurious and obviously catered for the rich, but as the tram proceeded between the two squares there was a marked change in the character of the town. After the University had been passed, the shops became more utilitarian. There were small *tavernas* instead of big restaurants where people stood at the counters to eat and kebabs turned on spits in the windows and great dishes of moussaka steamed beside the dishes of stuffed tomatoes and syrupy cakes decorated with cinnamon and honey.

It was easier than she had thought to take a ticket to Piraeus on the underground railway, much easier in spite of the language difficulties than the London tube, for the train only ran in the one direction and Piraeus was the last stop. She sat on the wooden seat surrounded by dark-clad workmen. There seemed to be very few women travelling and she was conscious of the stolid stare of many expressionless black eyes.

When she got out at the station, however, and confidently gave her Greek lettering instructions to the nearest cab driver, a further difficulty confronted her, for he seemed unable to read it. But a friend of his came to the rescue and after much discussion they set off with Stacey hoping desperately that now she was heading for the Royal Hellenic Yacht Club but not in the least certain about it. But she need not have worried. The taxi ascended a circular driveway and drew up with a squealing of brakes in front of an imposing building flying the

Greek flag and set high over the yacht basin, with the blue sea beyond. A bed of huge pink pelargoniums flourished in the sea air and everything was bright and polished as if in the tradition of the navy itself.

The atmosphere inside was more in the style of a formal old-world institution than of a sailing club, for the furniture was grand and in heavy style, very luxurious and imposing. Stacey felt shy, for there was a hushed atmosphere and she did not know where to look for Niko. But a kindly woman who seemed to be a caretaker came to greet her and asked her in good English what she required, and she was directed into a room where a few people seemed to be taking an aperitif.

But the figure who rose to greet her was not Niko. Her heart quivered as she recognized the saturnine features and unsmiling face of the elder brother – Stavros. What was he doing here?

'I told Niko I would give you lunch here. I'm afraid he finds himself otherwise engaged and he asked me to explain. An old friend of his – a lady, need you ask – happens to be in Athens and he is anxious to see her. He is so sorry, but said he did not doubt that I would make a good substitute. What do you think, Stacey, will I do instead?'

He smiled at last and his whole face was transformed. But Stacey was confused and perturbed. Did Stavros really want to take her to lunch? His ideas of politeness were severe she knew and he would not let his brother appear discourteous. But what did he really feel about it? Was it just another duty? And did he wish it had been Lauren instead of Stacey? It was impossible to answer any of these questions when she looked at his mouth that wore once more the enigmatic expression of a Greek statue.

'Would you like to lunch at the quayside near the boats?' he asked.

'Yes, that sounds pleasant,' Stacey agreed.

She sat admiring the view of the circular harbour with its houses that climbed steeply up the slopes.

'I hope you had a successful morning's shopping,' Stavros said.

'Oh, yes. I bought beautiful clothes, but they all seemed dreadfully expensive. I feel so guilty about putting Sophia to so much expense.'

'Don't worry, I will see about that. After all, it was my son's goat which caused the disaster, I understand, and we can hardly have our guests suffering inconvenience.'

'Oh, but . . . I didn't know. I wouldn't want you to pay for the clothes.'

'Let us forget about it. It does not matter in the least.'

It did matter to Stacey. She was horrified to think that Stavros intended to pay for her new clothes, but she realized it would be impossible to argue with him.

They lunched at the quayside where there were tables under gay awnings. The waiter brought them a selection of hors d'oeuvres, large purple and green olives, dishes of tiny fried fish, small pieces of fried octopus, and *kephtedes*, small rissoles made of beans. With these Stavros drank ouzo but ordered a delicious drink for Stacey with the cool fresh tang of lemons. Next they ate fish *plaki*, a fish cooked with onions and tomatoes. Stacey felt she would always remember this meal, taken so informally in the shade of the bright awnings with the water lapping against the gleaming yachts a few yards away. There were boats of all kinds and descriptions, some wide and capacious, others sleek and narrowly streamlined. And there were sunbronzed people working on the boats, painting, hammering, working with the sails.

'I came here to give orders about our boat, *Katrina*. It came back here for repair, but we will need it soon for expeditions around the other islands. Would you like to see her?'

He led the way along the quay to a place where a large motor yacht was moored, a craft of extreme beauty.

'She looks better at sea with all sails flying,' Stavros told her. He spoke in Greek to the two men on board. 'It should be ready soon, and then we can make one or two trips on it. Are you a good sailor?'

'I think so,' said Stacey.

It was exciting and yet alarming to think of being in such close proximity with her host. Being on a yacht was a different matter from the Citadel of Swallows where sometimes she did not even see him until evening. She thought it might prove a strain to be in his company on a boat like this, however luxurious it might be. And it was luxurious. He led the way down some steps into the living quarters. There was a salon with raised dais surrounded with wrought iron for the dining table and built-in seats covered with cream leather. The long sofas built into the walls were covered in green dralon velvet and the carpeting was of soft piled gold. There were colourful modern pictures on the walls and several pieces of sculpture.

The bedrooms were beautiful, each with its own bathroom, one furnished in pale apple green and another with lilac quilting on the walls. But when at last she was shown his apartment, Stacey noticed that in spite of the obvious expensiveness of its appointments, there was a severity and masculine orderliness about it that seemed to fit in with her conception of the character of Stavros. She went to the table and stood looking down at the navigation charts.

'This is really your life,' she said, 'isn't it? The island and the vines are just a relaxation.'

He looked at her as if she had awakened his interest.

'That is intelligent of you, Stacey. Yes, this is my life. You could say, my love. Everything to do with shipping has been my interest since I was a boy only as old as Socrates. I am happy when I am on this yacht. And yet the other smaller one suits me better. I like to be on my own in a small boat, navigating by the stars and the sun, but my business interests are such that I cannot be spared to make a journey as long as I would like. Unfortunately we have to live in the jet age. The age of sail has become a luxury to be indulged in only at certain times.'

The cabin was smaller than the other compartments with a single bunk bed covered by a dark blue blanket. There was little room for his tall figure beneath the low ceiling and when he showed her a map of the Greek islands pointing out the ones she should see, it seemed to Stacey that he was very close to her in this small space. She sat down at the table and he bent down over her as he showed her the route they might take. Stacey was vividly aware of his arm brushing against her hair. How foolish she was to be affected so much by his proximity when he did not even seem to think of her as a woman, let alone an attractive one.

When she stood again they were very close and she forced herself to meet his eyes. What did she read there? For a moment there seemed to be a relaxation of the cool look that she had come to expect. She turned aside in case her own eyes should betray her and said the first thing that came into her head.

'Does Niko enjoy sailing?' she asked.

He seemed to be jerked back from some far-away region of the mind.

'Niko? Yes, he is quite useful with a boat. He excels at anything that requires a certain amount of daring and courage. As to your friend Colin, I could not say. I have not travelled with him yet. Have you?'

'Why do you ask that?'

She was thinking that he had deliberately drawn her attention to the fact that she was supposed to be engaged to Colin.

'Isn't it customary for young English people to travel together these days even before they marry? We see plenty of that in the islands.'

'And I suppose if I were a Greek girl that would not be approved of?'

'Most certainly not. We are very careful of our women.'

'And English girls are careful of themselves.'

'I am glad to hear it. But it does not always appear so.'

He had had the effect again of putting her in the wrong and making her so furious that she did not consider what she was saying. A moment ago she had been fascinated by those dark eyes, by the touch of his arm brushing against her hair, but now she was thankful that he had annoyed her. Now she could attempt to be sensible. Certainly it was the height of foolishness to consider herself attracted to this censorious man.

'Well, for your information, I have never travelled with Colin, as you put it. But if I wanted to, I would. I've told you before that English girls can look after themselves.'

'So much so that you travelled all the way to Paxados to make sure that Colin was behaving himself, isn't that what happened? You are just as possessive with the man of your choice as a Greek woman would be.'

She sighed with exasperation.

'It was chance that I had the opportunity to travel to Athens with Colin's sister. Naturally we wanted to see him while we were so near.'

'It does not become you to be angry, Stacey,' Stavros said. 'Your eyes, so brown and beautiful, should always be gentle.'

'Oh, Stavros!'

The compliment was so unexpected, coming in the midst of their angry dispute, that she was overwhelmed by the emotions that she had tried so hard to avoid. He seemed to sense this and put his hands on her shoulders, gently drawing her towards him. But while she yielded to her feeling of utter surrender to the will of a stranger who had enchanted her, there came a sharp knock at the door and it burst open. Stavros quickly dropped his hands and turned around as Niko strode into the cabin.

'Here you are, then! How fortunate that I found you. Popi had another appointment after lunch, so I came back to find Stacey. My humble apologies for breaking our date, my sweet. But I did not think you would object to Stavros for a substitute, and it seems I was not mistaken. What do you say, Stavros? Can I take this delightful young lady off your hands now or not?'

Stavros had recovered from the emotional moment — if there ever had been one — for Stacey wondered whether it had been created by her imagination and by her own attraction to this difficult man. Certainly he gave no sign of being disturbed as he turned to Niko saying, 'Of course, Stacey must come with you. It has been delightful entertaining her to lunch, but now I have other tasks to do. We will meet this evening at the house.'

She followed Niko to the place where he had parked his powerful dark green sports car and he held open the door for her.

'It's wonderful to drive again,' he said. 'You won't mind, Stacey, if I open her up?'

As soon as they were installed in the car, he switched on the radio and Greek *bouzouki* music floated out at them. He seemed to be a skilful driver, but Stacey had one or two moments when she wondered whether they would reach Athens alive, for he had the verve and audacity that is associated with driving a powerful car of this kind. He took frightful risks, she thought, cutting in, overtaking, trying to and usually succeeding in beating the traffic lights. They drove quickly along the splendid seafront boulevards and reached streets that were crowded with bicycles, motor scooters, trucks busy unloading their goods and taking up double space, not to speak of pedestrians leaping out of the way of all these vehicles.

They spent the rest of the afternoon rushing around the city at breakneck pace, and Stacey was confused and bewildered by the various sights he showed her — the

Plaka beneath the Acropolis with its streets of metal wares and strings of sandals hanging outside the shops, the Agora or covered market, where, because it was the Lenten season, there were stalls offering decorated candles, icons and containers which scented the air with the heavy fragrance of incense. This was a complete contrast to the smart hotel where they had cherry syrup and pastries and danced to a modern four-piece band.

She had to admit that Niko was very good company, though she could never take him seriously. His wicked eyes took in all the pretty girls in the hotel where they danced and he occasionally waved to one or another of his acquaintances.

'You seem to have lots of pretty girl-friends,' Stacey chaffed him. 'Isn't it time you settled down? Don't you know anyone who would make a good wife?'

'Quite a lot who would like the chance of trying,' laughed Niko.

'How conceited you are! Are all Greek men like you?'

'Heaven forbid! But Stavros is serious enough for the two of us. Not that he was always like that. Before he married he was cheerful enough. Maybe that is why I have kept single. It is fatal to give your heart to a woman. Don't you agree?'

'How can I? Was Maria very lovely?'

'Exquisite.'

The one word stabbed Stacey unexpectedly so that she gasped for breath. How foolish to have this reaction! How could it hurt her because she heard praise for a woman who had died tragically a long time ago?

The house in a quiet square of Athens was beautifully furnished with antiques, its hallway and staircase carpeted in forest green, the walls of gold damask wall-paper. Stacey was shown to the room she was to share with Lauren by Cassandra, a severe-looking house-keeper who looked as if she merited Sophia's description of her as a dragon. They were to meet Hélène later before going out to dine.

Lying in a scented bath, Stacey thought over the busy events of the day. She found herself looking forward very much to the evening when they were all to dine together. And her dress with the Pucci print was lying on her bed all ready and beautiful enough to wear any-where. Lauren arrived just as she had finished her bath.

'I'm quite dead,' she declared, looking very much alive with her vibrantly lovely hair and sparkling green eyes. 'They worked me like a dog, but we got some very successful shots, and I wore the most way-out clothes. Am I looking forward to that bath! Be a dear, Stacey, and run it for me, will you?'

Afterwards, as she sat in front of the wide mirror, Lauren glanced around the large room with its deep turquoise carpet and exquisite hangings of pale silk.

'It would be wonderful to be married to a Greek ship-owner,' she mused. 'What do you think of Stavros, Stacey, do you like him any better?'

'Yes, I think I do. I had lunch with him today.'

Lauren looked a little annoyed.

'Really, Stacey, you seem to be making a habit of it. What happened to Niko?'

'He couldn't come, so Stavros met me instead.'

Lauren looked relieved. 'Oh, so Stavros with his polite Greek manners took over. Kind of him. Did you spend the afternoon with him?'

ᶠ 'No, Niko came back.'

'Stavros must have been pleased. I know he said he was going to be frightfully busy. Stacey, you aren't really interested in either of them, are you?'

Stacey reflected that even if she was she would never tell Lauren.

'But I know you aren't. If you're interested in anyone, it's Colin. That's unfortunate. But I wanted to ask you about tonight,' Lauren continued, as she proceeded to apply gold eyeshadow to her lids. 'Please try to take over Niko and give me a chance with Stavros. One so seldom gets a chance to have him on his own on the island. I'm sure he's really interested, but I need some more time to work on him. Won't you engage Niko's interest? It won't be hard to do. He's a terrific one for a pretty girl, and you're looking gorgeous in that new dress.'

In spite of Lauren's instructions, Stacey felt thrilled at the prospect of an evening in Athens when eventually they were sitting in the silver Rolls. 'I will drive the hearse,' Niko had said, 'and Stacey can sit beside me. I know I made her nervous this afternoon and now I will show her how sedately I can drive if I wish to.'

Stavros and Lauren took the back seat, and Stacey reflected that this was to be the pattern of the evening. She was conscious that she looked lovely in her new silk dress and she had done her hair in a more sophisticated fashion. The Greek sandals she had bought that afternoon were of thonged silver and she wore silver filigree ear-rings. Lauren was dressed in black, a wisp of a dress that showed off her beautiful shoulders and legs. She had an elegant air that drew attention away from all other women. She was at her most charming this evening and Stavros was being given the full benefit of her poise. Now Stacey saw a different side of him, an urbane, suave man with beautiful manners intent on showing a beautiful woman the night life of the city.

They came to the Plaka, for Lauren, hoping to please Stavros with a taste for real Greek life, had chosen to come here to dine rather than go to one of the restaurants in the Syntagma Square area. The Plaka was the old part of Athens beneath the Acropolis and Stacey had already seen something of it with Niko during the afternoon, but at night it seemed entirely different, though still like a village preserved in the heart of a city, with its steep roads and stairways, its small shops and *tavernas* pouring out the smell of delectable food together with their plangent music.

The smoky *taverna* where they chose to eat was full of noise and life. There was a four-piece band with violin, zither, pipe and concertina clashing out the vibrant tunes of Greek folk songs. At the back of the place a lamb was turning on a spit and soon they were eating tender pieces of this meat spiced with oregano and flavoured with lemon.

There was a space cleared for dancing and every now and again some man would get up and start dancing in a slow feline rhythm, then others would join him and a group of people would circle the floor with arms entwined. Stacey felt relaxed and happy, even though it was Niko who was pressing her to drink retsina, Niko who was urging her to join in the dance. She had made up her mind that she must try to forget the strange feelings she had when she was with Stavros. He was not for her, that was certain. With a man like him someone like Lauren had much more chance. And Lauren was revelling in his company. In the blue smoky atmosphere, she leaned across the small iron table and put her hand on his arm, gazing into his enigmatic dark eyes with a laughing, enchanting expression in those almond-shaped eyes that gave off the brilliance of a clear emerald.

When they came out of the *taverna* about an hour before midnight, the moon was full, shedding its silver gleam upon the narrow streets, the small quiet squares with their old houses decorated with Corinthian designed pillars and roofs of russet tiles now colourless in the pervading light.

'Now we must show our visitors the ultimate vision, the Acropolis by moonlight,' Niko declared, and he drove the car to the place beneath the rock where hanging above, like a ship in full sail, the great temple stood floodlit against the dark blue of the sky. Under the additional enchantment of the full moon, it had become a palace of ice, the marble reflecting a silver glow and casting deep velvet shadows.

Their shoes were not meant for the steep climb up the path, but Stacey would not have missed it for anything. Niko took her arm and they went ahead with Lauren and Stavros following along the worn pathway. Ahead, clear in the silver light, was the Parthenon, its immense columns appearing to rise from the rock as if floating in the air. They stood upon the limestone slabs and gazed at the soaring colonnades. There were a few visitors around, but this was hardly noticeable, for they were like shadows in this ghostly light and voices were hushed. Beneath them the lights of Athens shone as far as Mount Lykabettos. From here the whole city could be seen spreading out towards the sea and the distant hum of traffic drifted upwards like the drowsy murmur of summer bees.

The night breeze blew cool on this high place and Stacey shivered. Immediately she was enfolded by Niko's arm.

'Are you cold? We must keep you warm.'

Stavros and Lauren were talking quietly together. Stacey could hear his deep musical voice and the husky tones used by Lauren when she wanted to be at her most alluring. Occasionally there was a low laugh. Obviously they were getting on well together. Stacey was so absorbed in her own thoughts that she was hardly aware of the man at her side, and he seemed to sense this.

'You are very quiet. What is it? Is the Parthenon by moonlight a little too overwhelming for you?'

No, it is beautiful.'

She tried to shake off the depression she felt at the thought of Lauren succeeding in arousing the interest of Stavros.

'I've loved the whole day,' she declared to Niko. 'It's all been absolutely wonderful. Thank you so much for showing me your city.'

'Ah, that's better,' he said, smiling. His hand caressed her arm and brought her closer to him. Niko was so pleasant that she could not find it in her heart to repulse him, although she was conscious that Stavros and Lauren were close by and that above all she did not want Stavros to think she was flirting with his brother.

She was surprised, however, when Stavros said, 'We had better go if we are to make an early start tomorrow. Niko, watch Lauren and I will help Stacey back to the path.'

He took her arm and they slowly made their way

down. She had not bargained for the effect his nearness had upon her. In the moonlight of this magic place she felt overwhelmed by the presence of this man who himself looked like one of the senators who had walked on this hill long ago. His expression was unreadable, his eyes dark and expressionless as if, like those of the ancient statues, they were made of onyx.

But now he turned to her. 'You must not take my brother too seriously. He is inclined to take advantage of any situation which involves being in romantic surroundings with a pretty girl.'

'Of course, I realize that,' she replied a little sharply. 'I'm not entirely without sense.'

'I'm glad to hear it. Even though you consider yourself betrothed to Colin, I thought it best to warn you.'

Stacey felt she could not argue. What use was it to deny her engagement to Colin? He was determined to believe it because it suited him. And as for Niko, surely he did not think she was trying to charm him?

'I assure you,' she said, 'I can look after myself. And I have no ideas about Niko, so you needn't worry about that.'

'Good,' he said.

She was so annoyed by this short abrupt response and the contrast between their conversation and the way she was feeling as he led her down the steps with the lights of Athens all below them, and the beautiful Parthenon above, and his hand warm on her arm, that she said, 'Really, Stavros, the sooner I can leave Paxados the better. I think you'd better consider releasing me from the agreement to teach Socrates.'

'We will see about that,' he replied. 'You don't want to spoil Lauren's plans, do you? If you go, Lauren will go too.'

So that's it, Stacey thought. He wants to keep me here because he too is interested in developing this relationship with Lauren. He only separated me from Niko because he didn't approve of seeing me with Niko's arm around me and thought he'd better rescue his brother from my clutches.

And Lauren had similar thoughts. She waltzed around the bedroom when they had returned looking quite lovely in her silk nightdress that was in a white Grecian design banded under the breasts with gold, but pouting at Stacey and saying, 'Why did you encourage Niko to flirt with you? Stavros has such a sense of responsibility towards his guests and felt he must separate you.'

Stacey forbore to tell her that she had previously instructed her to gain attention from Niko so that she herself could be free to attract Stavros.

'But no matter. There's plenty of time yet, and tonight Stavros seemed really interested in me. I have high hopes that if I stay here a week or two more I'll have him eating out of my hand.'

Stacey sighed. The picture this conjured up was so opposite to her ideas of Stavros. She had become used to the disapproval of this stern man, though she admitted he had devastating charm. She could never in her wildest dreams imagine he would eat from her hand.

CHAPTER NINE

IT was good to be on Paxados again, almost like coming home. No more was said about Stacey's departure and she resumed her informal lessons with Sox. The days drifted past as if in a pleasant dream. Stacey tried to avoid meeting Stavros more than was necessary because she was afraid her feelings towards him would increase. It was a bitter-sweet situation, especially as she had to listen to Lauren speaking about the progress she hoped she was making with him.

Colin had begun to pay Stacey more attention in public, but Stacey thought this was to serve as a disguise for his real interest in Alexandra. It did not worry her, for she had long ago recovered from all interest in him. Chrysoula seemed more temperamental than ever, but this now took the form of moodiness and sulks. She was not so flamboyant in her antagonistic attitude to Stacey. Perhaps, Stacey thought, she had realized where Colin's true interests lay.

The weather was becoming warmer now. Greek households, Stacey had found, seemed to have no sense of time. It did not seem to matter whether one had meals punctually or not, and yet whatever time the family decided to lunch or dine the food was always perfect, piping hot or ice cold, and cooked beautifully. Today she had taught Sox during the morning and they had subsequently bathed. Then they had lingered over cool long drinks under the vines in the courtyard and finally had a long slow delicious lunch of iced soup and small

crayfish followed by melon filled with wild straw-
berries.

The delicate white wine had made Stacey a little
sleepy and for once, unusually for her, she decided to
take advantage of the siesta time. Lauren had stayed
behind talking to Stavros, so Stacey decided that rather
than risk being disturbed later she would sleep out on
the verandah beyond the bedroom with its slatted blinds
that cast a green reflection of sunshine and shade on to
the comfortable chaise-longue with its yellow cushion.
The shadows of the swallows were reflected on the blind
and she dozed off hearing the cicadas shrilling with a
continuous note from a nearby tree. She was not aware
that she had slept for very long when she heard the door
close and the sound of voices from the bedroom.

First there was Lauren. 'It's all right, Stacey isn't
here. She doesn't usually sleep in the afternoon. I told
you we'd be quite alone here.'

Stacey sat up. She was befogged with sleep but aware
that she must either declare her presence now or keep
quiet. But she was frozen with confusion, for she
thought the other person might be Stavros. But surely
Lauren would never bring Stavros to her room. He was
so strict in his attitude to his guests and in preserving
convention. It could not be him. Stacey's hesitation was
her undoing, for now it was too late to interrupt. Colin's
voice said, 'Lauren, you must help me. I'm in a jam.'

'What, again? Oh, really, Colin!' said Lauren's cool
voice.

'But this time it's serious.'

'And other times? Well, Colin, what is it?'

'I need money desperately.'

'Oh, heavens, Colin, that's nothing new.'

'But it affects you, too. You've got to help me. It will be to your advantage too to keep in favour with Stavros. Don't think I'm not aware of your little plans too.'

'What of it?'

'I'm getting on well with Alexandra. You know that.'

'Yes, but you will have to get the approval of Stavros. You do realize, Colin, that there can't be any funny business with a girl like that?'

'Of course I do, and that's why I'm desperately anxious to put things right.'

'What things?'

'Chrysoula.'

'Oh, lord!' Lauren's voice conveyed a wealth of meaning.

'It isn't what you think – at least it isn't now. But I must admit I had an affair with her that went the whole way. How could I help it? She was damned attractive and not unwilling. But now she's threatening to tell Stavros. It would ruin my chances with Alexandra if she knew. She's just a child, but you know how fiery she can be. And Stavros – I haven't got a chance if he finds out. You know what Greeks are like about women having to be virtuous, especially in the islands. No, the only solution is to get her away.'

'But would she go?'

'Willingly. She's dying to go and work in Athens. She thinks it's the next best thing to going to America. In fact that will probably be her next ambition. But at the moment she'll be satisfied with Athens. Only she needs money to get there and to keep herself for a while. It isn't much she's asking for, but I just haven't got it. Even taking Alexandra to *tavernas* here has cleaned me out. I had an advance from Stavros long ago. I can't ask for more. It would get me even more into disfavour.'

'And what do you want me to do?'

'Lend me some money, of course. You must still have plenty from your fashion assignment.'

'Are you crazy? I only have enough to get home. I spent what I earned in Athens on some fabulous new clothes. I'm making my plans for the future too, you know.'

'Damn it all, there must be some way! You've always helped me before.'

'I wonder if Stacey has anything,' mused Lauren.

'I don't know about that. I don't think she can have much.'

'Couldn't you be a bit nice to her? She used to think you were marvellous. Maybe she still does.'

'Yes. Pity about that – she's a sweet thing. But love in a cottage wouldn't suit me. In any case, I can't ask her for any more. I still owe her something from when I first came here.'

'Oh, God, Colin, you don't! I didn't know that. She never told me. What are we to do, then?'

'Perhaps you could ask her. Say you've run short because of your shopping in Athens. After all, she's the only one who has any prospects of earning money at the moment, with teaching Sox.'

'But you have too. You still do the library work. Couldn't you get an advance?'

'I've had one already. I can't ask for more. No, the only thing is to get Stacey to ask for some salary on account. We can pay her back when you're working again.'

'I like that! You mean *I*'ll have to pay her back. Honestly, Colin, you are the end!'

'But if this thing blows up on me, it will affect you too, don't you realize? You won't be popular with Stavros if your brother is in hot water. Money really is a damn curse when you haven't got it. When I think of all the money that the Demetrios family have! And I'm in a fix for want of a few hundred drachma.'

'All right, I'll ask Stacey. She seems to be quite in favour with Stavros.'

'Oh. You're sure she isn't on the same trend of thought as you are, Lauren darling?'

'I shouldn't think so. Even if she is, I don't think she has a hope. A man like Stavros would go for someone more sophisticated.'

'Like you, you hope. Oh, well, I wish you luck.'

'He's terribly attractive. That, and all the lovely money.'

'We're both fortunate. I must say I find Alexandra has something too. Of course, she's very young, but time will improve that. I swear if I can marry her there won't be any more girls like Chrysoula.'

There was quiet in the room. Evidently Colin had gone. Stacey heard Lauren moving around and then the slight creak of the bed as she lay down. She herself remained on her chaise-longue thinking over the conversation she had just heard. Well, at least now, when Lauren approached her, she would know what it was all about. But what an idea! How could she possibly approach Stavros for money? Her whole being cringed at the thought. They must find some other way.

When she had made sure that Lauren was sleeping, she tiptoed from the room. They must not know she had overheard the conversation. But she was determined, however charmingly Lauren put her case, that she would not yield to persuasion.

She had taken her swimsuit, a bright yellow bikini, which flattered the golden tan of her smooth skin, and now she made her way down the path to the little private beach where there was a changing room set in a grove of old wind-racked olive trees. She had thought she would have the little bathing beach to herself, but when she walked towards it she heard the sound of voices raised in gay chatter, the high childish voice of Sox and a deep resonant voice that she would know anywhere. She paused, feeling that perhaps she was intruding, for she had never before seen Stavros alone with his son.

He was coaching him in swimming strokes in the clear shallow water of the bay. They were utterly absorbed in their task, very serious and touchingly similar. For the first time, Stacey saw how much the boy resembled his father, the classical features, and, when he had received a word of praise – the warm, enigmatic smile. But now Sox saw her and shouted, 'Stacey! Come and watch me. I can do a hundred strokes now easily. Soon I will be able to swim out to the yacht.'

In the bay the small boat was anchored. It was the same one in which Stavros had taken Stacey for a sail.

'Soon you will do that,' said Stavros. 'But now I think you have had enough for one day. You had better go and change. It's only springtime yet and the water is still not very warm.'

'I have to find Flavia too. She is always missing these days. Dimitraki said he would help me. Why do you think she wanders away so much?'

'She is getting older. She too feels springtime in her blood,' Stavros said.

He smiled at Stacey warmly and naturally and she was taken aback by the rush of emotion in her heart. How she wished this smile was really for her – but it was caused by his tender feeling for his little son, she knew. It was how any parent smiles at an onlooker as if to say, 'Haven't I got a fine child?'

When Sox had run away, hopping and skipping up the path between the gnarled olives, Stavros turned to her and said, 'Do you feel capable of swimming out to the boat? If you do, we could make some tea and be English for a change. I keep a supply on board.'

'That would be fun,' said Stacey.

It was no effort to swim in this smooth sea. The water was so clear that you could see stones on the bottom and groups of sea-urchins, those prickly round creatures whose coral-coloured interiors are considered a delicacy. They swam together in a leisurely fashion and Stacey was very happy to give herself up to the tranquillity she experienced as she swam by the side of this man whom she realized now she had begun to like very much. The joy of cleaving through the cool water, the benevolent warmth of the sun, brought a sense of wellbeing. And when they reached the rope ladder swung over the side of the small yacht she was sorry they had reached journey's end for the time being.

There were four steps down to the cabin and a swing-ing gas stove in a tiny galley just off the place where there was a single bunk.

'As you see, I don't cater for company,' said Stavros. 'Usually I use this boat when I wish to be alone.'

He put on the kettle and produced tea and powdered milk with a tin of biscuits from the small neat cupboard. Stacey was intrigued by this further glimpse of the different facets of his personality. He seemed so remote from the sophisticated man who had entertained them in Athens. The sun was warm in the closed cabin, but he produced a large towel for her to wrap around the bikini. And she was glad of this, for she had felt self-conscious in the confined space. He left her to dry herself while he went on deck, then came back to make the tea, having put on a cotton sweater. They sat on the bunk in companionable silence, drinking from the steaming mugs and munching the biscuits that were crisp and delicious from the newly opened tin.

'How are you getting on, now?' asked Stavros after a while. 'No regrets that you did not decide to go when you wanted to?'

Stacey did not know how to reply. Quite truly she regretted in some ways that she had stayed on the island, for every day brought her feelings more clearly before her. She was very much attracted now to this man who constantly awed and yet delighted her. And what was she to do? She must succeed in concealing her feelings, because Lauren was the one who must attract him. Someone with as little experience as she herself could hardly have any charm for a man of the world like Stavros. Added to which there was the fact that he thought she was in love with Colin and hoped she was so that he could be sure Colin was not engaging the attention of Alexandra. It was all rather a muddle, and it would be best if she were to leave Paxados. Yet the thought of going away and never again seeing his dark eyes and his enigmatic smile filled her with dismay.

'I'm happy to give Socrates his lessons,' she compromised. 'He's a charming little boy.'

'I find him so. I'm afraid my business takes me away

137

from him a great deal. Sophia is very good with him, but in truth he needs someone he could regard as a mother.'

Stacey by no stretch of imagination could suppose that Socrates would ever regard Lauren as a mother, but she did not think this particularly important, for Sox was a very independent little boy and seemed to manage his own life very well.

'But surely, he thinks of Sophia as a mother.'

'Maybe. But Sophia is still young, comparatively. One day she will marry again. There are several old friends who would like to regard themselves as suitors for her hand. It is unfortunate that she is a little old for me. And of course we have been associated together for so long it would be like marrying one's sister.'

So he was thinking of marriage, Stacey pondered. Lauren therefore had a chance. She was glamorous, gay, sophisticated, lovely, and would make a perfect hostess. She seemed to fulfil every requirement for the wife of a man of the standing of Stavros.

'Socrates is an independent little boy,' she said, voicing her previous thoughts. 'I don't think he particularly needs female companionship. But of course I suppose it would be good for him to have someone near who was fond of him, and you say Sophia may not always be here.'

'So on the whole it is your considered opinion that I should marry again,' said Stavros. She looked at him a little startled, then saw he was teasing her. His smile was gay and without the enigmatic quality that constantly puzzled her.

'If you find someone you love then I would say it would be best for you to marry. But I speak without experience,' she replied.

He rowed her back in the small dinghy that belonged to the boat and took leave of her on the shore, for he intended to spend some time on the boat making a few adjustments to the mast. She would have liked to stay to help him, but he did not suggest it. It was clear that this was a hobby that he enjoyed alone, far removed from his hectic business commitments.

She made her way to the changing room and was surprised to find Alexandra there. She had evidently been for a bathe and was now in a towelling jacket drying her long dark hair.

'Have you been bathing alone?' asked Stacey, rather surprised.

'Yes,' Alexandra pouted. Her dark skin glowed against the chalk-white gown and her eyes were brilliant with the eyebrows arched like the wing of a bird. 'Colin is being difficult. He says he must be conscientious about the library work because he needs to be in favour with Stavros. Isn't it tiresome?'

'It seems sensible enough,' Stacey said, reflecting that Colin must be serious to have thought this out so far. Usually he followed his own desires without any thought of the future.

'I know now,' Alexandra went on, 'that I shouldn't have spoken to you as I did. Colin is in love with me only. He has never been properly in love with anyone else. And, Stacey, he is the only one for me.'

'But, Alexandra dear, you're so young. And you must have your family's approval.'

'Yes, I know, but Stacey, believe me, if I can't have Colin I will do something desperate, I swear. Run away or drown myself. We Greek women don't do things by half measures.'

Stacey was worried when she thought of this conversation. Alexandra was a child still and it was foolish, she supposed, to take her seriously, but she had sounded so much in earnest. What would she do if she knew about Chrysoula? Perhaps it would be good for Colin to marry Alexandra. It seemed he could make her happy and he had said himself that he wanted nothing better than to marry her and if he could do this he would never look at anyone else. So when Lauren approached her about borrowing the money she was not quite so adamant as she had intended to be. She brushed aside Lauren's attempts to explain the need with her own confession.

'I heard you and Colin talking. I know what it's about.'

Lauren looked rather taken aback.

'You did? Perhaps that's just as well. You must realize how important it is to Colin. It's not much he needs, and I'll see that you get paid back, I promise.'

'But how can I possibly ask Stavros for an advance? Honestly, Lauren, it's expecting a lot of me. Why can't you ask Niko?'

'Because I haven't any excuse. I'm not working for Niko. If I ask him for money it will sound like an immoral proposal to a Greek. And then I won't stand a chance with Stavros. I can't spoil things at this stage by bringing in the question of money.'

'And what about me? What will he think of me?'

'But you'll be going soon. It doesn't matter to you.'

Stacey was torn in different directions. She could not bear to think of Alexandra enduring heartbreak and doing something desperate.

'Colin is serious about Alexandra,' Lauren went on. 'I've never known him so in earnest about a girl. Chrysoula flung herself at him. You could hardly blame a man in the circumstances. And now for want of a little money it will ruin his chances and Alexandra's happiness. Please do it for us, Stacey. It can't affect you.'

Reluctantly Stacey agreed. But the decision weighed heavily on her conscience and she went around for the rest of the day feeling very depressed that she had promised to do something she thought unwise. And how was she to ask Stavros? It would be most embarrassing. The opportunity came sooner than she had expected, for that evening after dinner Stavros proposed that they should take a trip to Santorin in a few days' time on the large yacht. Stacey thought that this would provide an excuse for asking for the advance. She could say she had some idea of buying souvenirs there, that she needed money for possible expenses. The drawback to borrowing money, of course, apart from her natural embarrassment, was the fact that once she had done so she would not be at liberty to leave when she wanted to.

After breakfast she steeled herself to go and knock at the door of the study, and quaked inside herself as she heard the deep musical voice bid her enter. When nervously with a voice that she could not keep steady she had made her request, she managed to look at Stavros. He was smiling as if he wished to put her at her ease, and yet there was a little puzzled frown there too.

'I should have realized before that you might need an advance,' he said. 'I suppose the visit to Athens was rather a drain on your available money.'

'Yes,' said Stacey, blushing. The visit to Athens had cost her the price of a tram fare and an underground ticket, together with the price of a taxi from the station to the Yacht Club. Except that she had bought a pair of very reasonably priced sandals, it could hardly have cost less. She felt terribly ashamed to be asking for money when Sophia, in fact Stavros himself, had replaced her clothes so generously.

'I will arrange it straight away. I suppose it would be easier for you if I gave you cash instead of a cheque.'

'Oh, yes, please,' said Stacey. All she wanted to do was to get out of the study and away from those quizzical dark eyes and the small smile that played on the curving lips. She gave the money to Lauren, who said she would pass it on to Colin. She had asked Lauren not to say it had come from her, but Lauren had refused.

'Are you mad?' she demanded. 'If Colin thinks it came from me we'll never get it back. At least if he knows he owes it to you, he might return it. In fact I'll see that he does.

'Colin will arrange with Chrysoula that she goes to Athens while we're on the trip to Santorin, then there won't be any difficulty,' she went on. 'I'm so looking forward to being on the yacht with Stavros. What a pity you're not attracted to Niko, Stacey. It would be delightful to have a shipboard flirtation with him at any rate. I'd consider it if I were you. But with Stavros I want more than that.'

The dinner was gay that evening, for they were all in a relaxed holiday mood looking forward to the trip to Santorin. It was only to last a couple of days, but Stacey was told that the island was very beautiful, unlike anything they had ever seen before. Colin and Alexandra seemed to be being careful not to spend too much time together in public at least. Colin had been asked to join the cruise to Santorin on account of Lauren and Stacey so presumably he did not want to do anything that would spoil the plan.

At last, unable to bear the separation any longer, Alexandra jumped up and put a dance tune on the record player and she and Colin were able to be close even if their behaviour had to be circumspect. Stacey reflected that they need not have worried too much, for Lauren was engaging the attention of Stavros, as she danced with him to a slow romantic melody. Stacey sat talking quietly to Sophia, but finally, unable to go on seeing the elegant copper bronze head and the shining dark one so close together, she excused herself and went up towards her room. On the way there, however, she was diverted by a call from the direction of Socrates's room.

'Stacey, I can hear Flavia. I put her in the stable for the night, but someone must have let her out. Do you think I could go to fetch her? Otherwise she will stray, and I want to be sure she is here when we go tomorrow.'

Stacey looked at the sparkling dark eyes and the thin brown body covered only by a pair of short pyjama trousers.

'No. It's time you were asleep ... I'll go to find Flavia. She knows me now and it will be easy to see her in the moonlight.'

Socrates seemed quite contented to leave the task to her. Stacey covered him up with a warm blanket, for the night had turned a little chilly, then she went to her room to change into slacks and a pullover. It was almost as clear as day, with the moon painting its path of silver across the Aegean sea. At night sounds that were not noticeable during the day seemed clear and near at hand, and this was what had probably made Flavia restless. There was the continual sound of dogs barking in the village below and the melancholy braying of a donkey somewhere close by. But further up the slopes there sounded the tinkling of bells from the sheep and goats that wandered on the grass, restless because of the brilliance of the night.

Sounding close but higher up the path, Stacey thought she could hear the distinctive silvery sound of the bell that they had bought for Flavia only the other day, and she could even hear the sharp sound of her dainty hooves upon the stony path. The little animal was probably making for the citadel above the house, for she often went there with Sox. Stacey had seen the little boy lying on his stomach with the white kid alongside, his arm about her, gazing at the coastline and at the further islands that dotted the Aegean.

She had brought the lead with her to attach to Flavia's red collar, but it was not until she reached the stony pinnacle where the marble columns glistened in the silvery light that she saw the little animal standing like a small statue framed by the broken archway. She went towards her quietly calling her name, but Flavia was in a skittish mood. She watched Stacey approaching and then when she was within touching distance she leaped away and with a flick of her white tail she was off, running a little way and then coyly peering out from behind another broken pillar.

The game that Flavia had decided to play went on for some time and Stacey began to be quite breathless and a little impatient. At last, with much persuasion, she prevailed upon the kid to allow herself to be caught and tied to a pillar while she herself sat and rested after her exertions. It was so lovely in this high place. The other islands looked like ethereal castles instead of the shapes of rock that appeared during the day, and the night had an atmosphere of luminous moonlit enchantment.

She leaned against the pillar and closed her eyes, dazzled by the beauty of her surroundings and the sad, disquieting emotion she felt when she thought of Stavros. And when she opened her eyes, he was there. He seemed to have materialized as if by magic and was standing within a few yards of her.

'So there you are. Socrates told me you had gone in search of Flavia. You should have called me to come with you.'

Stacey, regarding his face that was ivory-coloured in the moonlight, the hair ebony, the eyes shining black onyx, thought that he was the last person she would have asked to accompany her. Now that he was here, she felt weak and helpless, confused by the emotions that she always felt in his presence.

'Surely it's safe to go out alone on the island at night?' she asked.

'Safe enough, I suppose. Safer than the streets of Athens. The islanders themselves are law-abiding. Unlike some of our more modern friends, they have a great respect for women. But anything could have happened to you. You could have fallen down into a ravine or have stumbled and received a sprain or have come to any kind of harm walking alone at night. Socrates had no right to send you out after this tiresome animal which can quite well look after itself.'

'He wanted to make sure she was safe before he goes off tomorrow,' said Stacey, caressing Flavia's silky pate. 'And he didn't ask me to come. I volunteered to find

Flavia.'

'You must not think because you are employed to teach Socrates that you are to be at his beck and call night and day. I don't want him to be spoiled. Goodness knows, Sophia does enough of that.'

'He's a nice little boy and not easily spoiled, I would say,' said Stacey, nettled by his assumption that she was indulging Sox.

She started to stand up preparing to go, and at the same time Stavros stepped forward to help her. He took her hand to draw her to her feet and suddenly, unexpectedly, she was in his arms, and he was kissing her, while the earth and sky seemed to swing in a kaleidoscope of dazzled brilliance to the tune of her fast-beating heart.

His arms dropped to his sides and she stumbled a little, but he made no attempt to steady her.

'I am sorry, Stacey. Sometimes a moonlit night and a pretty girl play strange tricks with a man. It won't happen again, I promise. I regret very much that it happened at all.'

CHAPTER TEN

It had been a sudden impulse on the part of Stavros, regretted as soon as he had yielded to it. He had said as much himself. But that did not stop Stacey from spending a sleepless night reliving the few moments when she had surrendered herself to the dangerous emotions that had swept over her when she was in his arms.

Over and over again she told herself that it had meant very little to him. It was natural that a man like him, who had been married to a lovely woman and had been deprived of love for so long, should be seized by a sudden attraction on a night of such magical quality as the one they had experienced. She must put behind her the feelings that had been aroused, for she knew that was what he would want. He had said as much. The scene had meant nothing to him. It would have been a different matter if he had been in Lauren's company. Perhaps it had happened because he had been feeling amorous to Lauren earlier during the same evening. However that might be, the only emotions he showed afterwards were of regret and contrition. He could not know that he had shattered Stacey's world and that to her the kiss had made clear how deep her feelings were towards him.

He had asked her to forget it and she had promised she would, but she knew that was not going to be easy. She could only pretend and go on living her normal life while inside her heart was aching. She was glad they were to have the distraction of the trip to Santorin, and yet sorry in a way, for it meant she was to see more of Stavros than usual.

They sailed next day from the island and it was as lovely as she had been promised, skimming over the calm sea that was like silk shot with the colour of emeralds and sapphires. The wind was brisk and soon they stopped using the engine with which they had cleared the harbour and hoisted the sails to catch the freshening breeze. The cabins were small but luxurious, each with its own tiny bathroom. Stacey's was decorated in pale green and gold and in Lauren's the hangings were of peach-coloured shantung.

Lauren and Alexandra changed into bikini costumes as soon as they had unpacked and lay in a sheltered place on the deck soaking up the warm sun that poured down from the cloudless blue sky. The passage of the boat over the smooth sea left a bubbling white wake and behind this came the dolphins leaping out of the water and regarding the humans with curious eyes, their mouths with their smiling appearance, giving an appearance of extreme benevolence. Socrates was fascinated by them.

'I wish I could have one for a pet,' he declared. 'Stavros told me that in the old days in Greece there were stories of boys playing with dolphins.'

'I hardly think Flavia would be pleased,' said Stacey.

She was wearing neat cream shorts with a striped top of green, brown and ivory and had tied her hair back with a green ribbon. Niko, arriving from his duties with the sails, declared she looked about sixteen.

'Doesn't she, Stavros?' he asked.

But Stavros, regarding the sails and calling an instruction to the man at the helm, did not appear to hear, though he gave her a cursory glance. Lauren called him and he went over to speak to her. Certainly Lauren did not look sixteen. She was wearing an exiguous swimsuit with tiny white lace pants and a brief covering of the same material across her lovely breasts. She seemed quite unconscious of the effect she had upon the members of the crew, who seemed to find excuses to pass the sheltered corner where she and Alexandra were sunbathing.

Stacey went on talking to Sox, trying hard to forget the small pain that seemed to be somewhere in the region of her heart. She must not be foolish, she told herself. Stavros was interested in Lauren, and her friend's elegance and sophistication certainly were qualities which a man of his way of living would need in a wife.

In the afternoon, the string of islands around Santorin appeared misty blue upon the horizon. The islands they had seen before had been attractive because of a harmony of colour and proportion and not because of scenic grandeur, but the approach to Santorin was quite different.

'It was the result of a volcanic eruption,' Sophia said. 'At first there were only a few rocks here. Then, about the time of the Trojan wars, a volcano rose from the sea forming a large island, but then there came a huge eruption and the middle of the island sank. Sea poured into the basin and formed a gulf with the fragments of the broken crater forming small islands. All kinds of things have happened since. Islands rise and then disappear. The volcano is still alive.'

Sox was looking around him with wide eyes.

'It won't go off while we are here, will it, Stacey?'

'Not today,' Stacey reassured him. 'I think the weather would be different if that were going to happen.'

They seemed to be sailing into a calm enclosed sea with small blue misted islands around. Ahead of them was Santorin itself, where a wall of rock rose sheer from the sea to where, thousands of feet above, a town of white houses was strung out along the top like some illustration of an enchanted village in a fairy tale. Between the sea and the town, winding its way up the cliff of red and black rock, was a zigzag path.

'You have to ride a mule if you want to see the town,' Sophia explained.

'What, all the way?' asked Lauren, who had put on an emerald green wrap and was standing to watch the approach to the island.

'I would advise you to change into slacks,' said Niko, 'sad as it is to lose the beautiful sight of Lauren in a swimsuit.'

'Are you going?' Alexandra asked Colin. They were standing silently as lovers do, their hands touching, but very discreetly.

'Of course,' said Sophia. 'Everyone must go. Even I will venture on one of these mules. They say they are very tame.'

'You are hopeful,' chaffed Niko. 'I have heard it said that they are the souls of the dead working their way from Purgatory by the task of climbing up that steep path. But from their behaviour on a previous occasion, I would say they are more like escaped fiends out of Hell.'

When she had been lifted none too gently on to the

back of one of the mules, Stacey felt inclined to agree.

'Hold the reins loosely,' yelled Niko, but already he was far behind. Stacey's mule, encouraged by her light weight, pranced up the zigzag path, wavering from side to side, lurching, sprinting, sometimes going into a gallop, and when the fancy took it, leaping against the barrier wall as if trying to dislodge its passenger and flinging her into the sea. Stacey held on. As the uphill journey lengthened, she could see the yacht far below like a toy on the crawling silver reflections of the water. But finally she dared not look, for there was only this small wall between her and the downward drop and her mule seemed determined to edge as close to it as possible.

Her mule was ahead of all the rest and he kept his position. She ventured a look behind and caught a glimpse of Niko with Socrates in front of him on the saddle and of Sophia behind looking like a picture of the Wife of Bath with a hat swathed in a scarf upon her head. Then came Alexandra and Colin riding close together and finally Stavros and Lauren, trotting sedately, but with Lauren bending towards Stavros to make some remark.

Up and up they progressed, and at last Stacey began to enjoy it. The mule seemed to have given up trying to dislodge her and trotted briskly along the path, still wavering from side to side, but in a way that was a little less alarming, or else it could be that she was getting used to it. And then she found Stavros at her side.

'All right, Stacey?' he asked, and she nodded breathlessly, for the sight of him, carefree and laughing and in holiday mood, had once more brought back that thrilling feeling that she found it hard to suppress when in his company. At last they were far above the sea at the top of the sheer wall in the street of houses and shops that stretched like a row of giant's teeth along the topmost ridge of this strange island.

Up here the light was glorious and the other islands seemed to float around them in hazy splendour upon the calm blue of the sea. The sunshine upon the white walls turned them to the colour of liquid amber and all along the street that was paved with black and white marble, the wares hung outside the shops, brightly coloured rugs, creamy intricately patterned wool pullovers.

'Surely we've walked far enough,' said Colin when they came to a *taverna*. 'Let's stop for a drink or some coffee.'

Sophia and Lauren agreed since they knew they would have to walk down to the harbour again. *Bou-zouki* music was coming from its open doors and a few tourists were trying out dance steps with some of the local inhabitants. But Stacey felt she did not want to go in yet. She still wanted to see as much as possible of this place that looked almost as if it had only recently suffered the disaster of the eruption and yet was so strangely lovely.

'I think I'll walk a little more,' she said. And to her surprise, Stavros agreed with her.

'We can walk as far as the Cathedral,' he said. 'Then you can see the other side of the island. It's a strange contrast.'

Lauren looked displeased, but there was little she could do. She was being drawn into the dancing by Niko. Colin and Alexandra were sitting on a wall looking at the great vista of sea below them and trying to conceal the fact that they were holding hands. Socrates ran ahead skipping and jumping, then running back to pick up a marble pebble or make some remark to Stavros or Stacey. He was bubbling with joy at the opportunity to spend some time with his father. Stacey could sense his intense excitement and wondered whether she should try to calm him down a little.

After the radiant light of the out-of-doors, the Cathedral was dim and luminous with the pale light of tapers that shone on the golden ikons and holy pictures. It smelled of incense and flowers. But beyond was an open courtyard of arched white columns and far below could be seen the other side of the island.

'You can see it is a contrast,' said Stavros. 'You see, this cliff is the edge and the sea has filled in what was once the crater of the volcano. Beyond on the other side are the gentle green outer slopes of the mountain.'

It was as he said. There were vineyards on the slopes, a dramatic contrast to the high blackened cliff they had had to negotiate from the sea side.

'We will buy some wine for you to sample,' said Stavros. 'It's a good sweet wine, Vino Santo. It will be pleasant to have it with dinner when we leave.'

Stacey was happy in this moment of time. She did not think of anything but the present and that was wonderful, standing near Stavros amongst the white columns in the golden luminous air with the wide view of sea and islands spread below on the one side and the gentle slopes of young green vines on the other. And Socrates too made a part of her happiness as he danced like a small faun in and out of the white archways. She became conscious that Stavros was regarding her closely, though she found it hard to read the expression of his dark eyes.

'That's better, Stacey,' he said. 'You have been look-ing very wistful and sad during the last few days. I have noticed it. But now you look happier. What has made you so sad? Or should I not ask? Is it because Colin is again paying attention to Alexandra? If you take my advice I think you should reach some decision with this young man.'

She looked at him, quite taken aback by the fact that he had noticed her expression over a number of days. What could she say to him? Certainly not the truth, which was that his attentions to Lauren and the com-plete impossibility of her feelings towards himself had saddened her.

'Forgive me, I have made you look sad again.'

Nothing more was said and they walked back towards the place where the others were getting ready to make the journey down the steep path. It would be too hair-raising an experience to go downwards on the mules. They preferred to trust their own feet.

As soon as they had returned to the rest of the party, Lauren had started to talk to Stavros, commanding his attention entirely. Sophia had gone ahead, for she said she wanted to take it slowly, and she had taken Alex-andra and Niko with her, one on each side, for she was a little timid of the steep descent they had to make. Socrates was still full of energy in spite of all the exer-tions of the afternoon.

'When are you coming?' he demanded of Stavros, but his father frowned at his excited behaviour and told him sharply to calm down and behave himself. Sox looked crestfallen and Stacey said quickly, 'You must come down with me. I'm sure I'll need help.' Lauren seized this opportunity to demand that Stavros should accompany her and Stacey found herself left alone with Colin and Socrates. Just then one of the men in charge of the mules came down the path driving a few of them before him.

'I want to ride again,' said Sox.

'No, I don't think you'd better,' said Stacey, feeling a little worried about his excitable mood.

'Let the child ride if he wants to,' said Colin, lazily. 'He's used to riding donkeys all over Paxados. He won't come to any harm here.'

'I don't think he should. It's so steep.'

'The mule man will keep an eye on him. Let him go. I want to talk to you.'

Reluctantly Stacey yielded to his persuasion, and Sox was soon lost to sight on the bouncing white mule.

'Thank you for helping me over the fix I was in,' said Colin when they were alone. 'I'm truly grateful, Stacey. I haven't forgotten that I owe you the other money too. You shall have it back as soon as I can manage it.'

'Is everything all right about Chrysoula?' Stacey inquired.

'Yes, she was due to go to Athens while we were on this cruise. We thought it would be better if she made her departure as soon as possible.'

'But, Colin, shouldn't you have married her?'

'Are you crazy? It was only a short affair. Besides, she didn't want marriage as soon as she found out I had no money. She was under the illusion that all Englishmen are rich.'

'Are you going to marry Alexandra?'

'I hope so. Believe me, Stacey, she means more to me than I'd thought possible. I don't want anything to spoil it now. That's why I'm so grateful you could lend me the money.'

There was no chance for Stacey to reply to this, for suddenly they heard a commotion further down the pathway and a cry from Socrates, followed by sounds of people running and loud exclamations in Greek.

Stacey started to run. 'Something has happened!' she exclaimed, dismayed.

Around a bend of the path she came upon a little group of people. Stavros was bending over the still form of Socrates, who had been thrown from the mule, which had evidently careered wildly down the path, urged on by the excited little boy. The muleteer was trying to explain to Stavros, Stacey gathered, that it had not been his fault. Stavros looked as pale as the unconscious form of his son.

'It's dangerous to move him,' he said. 'Niko must ride for a doctor right away. There is one on the island. Colin, you go and borrow a blanket. We must keep him warm. Lauren, go back to the yacht. Tell Sophia, but don't let her come. She can wait for us on the boat. Stacey, you had better stay here. I might need help.'

The pleasant dream-like afternoon had suddenly changed into a nightmare. Stacey stayed with Stavros, cradling Socrates' head on her lap. She hardly felt the rough surface of the path or noticed the scratches that she had got upon her legs when she sat down too quickly in her haste to help.

'How did it happen that he was on a mule?' asked Stavros. 'I thought I made it clear that it was dangerous to ride down, especially for such a lightweight child.'

Stacey could only stare miserably at him in reply.

'I did not think it of you that you would neglect Sox just because you were in Colin's company.'

She realized he hardly knew what he was saying, for his anxiety was so great. But the bitter words were like the lashes of a whip as she gazed at the still face of the little boy whom she had grown to love so much in the past weeks.

CHAPTER ELEVEN

BACK at Paxados, although the doctor at Santorin had given a hopeful diagnosis, namely that Socrates had a little concussion and a broken ankle, Stavros had sent to Athens for a specialist who had been flown to the island by private plane. He gave much the same verdict and advised rest and no excitement. Sox had no choice but to follow these instructions, as his ankle was in plaster, and Stacey found it difficult to keep him occupied and happy, for he was usually such an active little boy.

It was Holy Week, and as Easter is the most important celebration in the Greek calendar, even more important than Christmas, Sophia was very occupied with household preparations, so Stacey had taken over Sox's nursing. There had been a coolness between her and Stavros since the accident. Stavros had made no apology for his angry words and Stacey thought he evidently considered it was true that she had neglected Sox because she wanted to talk to Colin.

Chrysoula had gone, but nothing had been said about it. Sophia must know, but probably Stavros was so concerned about Sox that he would never miss one of the servants. He did not even seem to notice, thought Stacey, that Colin and Alexandra were spending a great deal of time with each other, as if they thought they might be parted and must make up for this in the present.

Sox was a very demanding patient and Stacey had little time to think of anything else. Lauren looked in every now and then, but was obviously bored at the idea of entertaining a sick child, and, when Stavros was occupied, she went off with Niko to increase that wonderful tan that was making her look even more alluring.

The weather had become hot and during the late afternoon Sox became rather fractious, as his leg was paining him, so Stacey was glad when Stavros appeared and was welcomed very excitedly by his young son. Stacey rose to go, for she thought Stavros wanted to be alone with him, but Sox protested loudly, 'Why are you going, Stacey? I want you both here.'

'Perhaps Stacey would like to go,' said Stavros. 'She seems to stay with you a great deal.'

For the first time since the accident, it seemed, he looked full at Stacey, and what he saw seemed to surprise him. Stacey knew that she was looking tired, for she had herself noticed the blue shadows under her brown eyes and the paleness of her skin that only last week had been tanned and rosy.

'Stacey, what have you been doing to yourself? Or what has this small son of mine been doing?'

'I need Stacey to look after me. You must not send her away,' Socrates demanded imperiously.

'She looks as if she needs a rest from you. Have you been looking after him all the time? There was no need for that. It was not in our agreement.'

Stacey was taken aback. Did he think that she was doing this because he had lent her money?

'I . . . I'm fond of Sox. This is nothing to do with any agreement.'

'But look at you! Where is the healthy one who rode up the hill to Santorin? You must give Stacey some rest,' he said, turning to Sox. 'Chrysoula can stay with you for a while sometimes. She has little to do and can teach you Greek songs.'

Socrates pouted. 'I don't want Chrysoula, and in any case she has gone – Sophia told me so.'

Stavros frowned. 'Gone? Do you mean she has left this house?'

'Yes, she has gone to Athens. She told me long ago that she wanted to go. She said she will find a rich husband there.'

'Indeed? And how did she manage to find the money to get to Athens?' Stavros asked.

'I should think she got it from Colin. She was always friendly with him,' suggested Socrates.

Stavros said nothing further on the subject. He advised Stacey rather abruptly to go and have a rest. Stacey was worried about the conversation, for Stavros had looked displeased, but he hid his feelings successfully and began to talk to Sox.

However, Stacey thought she had not heard the last on the subject of Chrysoula, and she was right. That evening Alexandra and Colin had gone down to the *taverna* in the village to eat and Niko and Lauren had gone as well, so Sophia, Stavros and Stacey were there alone. The main course of the dinner was grilled fish, and Sophia apologized for the frugality of the meal, although Stacey was enjoying the fresh flavour of the red *barbouni*.

'They are so busy in the kitchen preparing for the Easter Festival,' she said. 'And although Chrysoula was rather lazy we miss even her extra pair of hands.'

'And what has happened to Chrysoula?' asked Stavros.

In the candlelight, his dark eyes were still and watchful as if something had led him to be suspicious. At least that was what Stacey thought, but then again it might have been that she was feeling guilty about the whole business.

'I thought you knew she'd gone to Athens. She has never been satisfied with working on Paxados and longs for the city lights. She said someone had given her enough money to live there for a while and she wanted to leave.'

'Strange! I wonder who could have provided her with the money, and with what object?'

He looked at Stacey and she was afraid to meet the gaze of those dark penetrating eyes. She looked away and felt a blush rising from her neck to her brow. After dinner Sophia excused herself, saying she was going to see if Sox had everything he needed and was settling down to sleep. Stacey offered to go, but Sophia said, 'No, you have done enough for one day. Stay and amuse Stavros.'

Stavros did not look as if he wished to be amused. He tapped with his knuckles upon the marble table, apparently deep in thought.

Finally he spoke. 'It's a beautiful night, Stacey. Let us walk to the citadel. I would like to talk to you.'

This was the last thing that Stacey desired, but she felt that when Stavros was in this mood she could hardly refuse. The night was very mild and the path was clear in the moonlight. It led to the broken columns glittering silver against the dark cobalt sea. A night bird winged startled from the grass, shouting its piercing cry, and all around them the crickets made a shrill clamour. There was a seat overlooking the wide view of the Aegean sea, and Stavros took her arm when they reached it and indicated that she should sit down. The touch of his cool hand upon her arm made her start nervously, but she made a great effort to recover her poise, for it was evident that Stavros intended to interrogate her upon the subject uppermost in his mind.

'It seems odd,' he said, 'that Chrysoula obtained enough money to set herself up in Athens. Certainly she was not the saving type. Her father often enough complained to me over her extravagance.'

Stacey was silent. There seemed no need to reply until it was strictly necessary. He turned towards her and as if to emphasize his concern he placed both hands upon her shoulders and turned her to face him. Why, she thought, did she feel this tremulous awakening to his touch, when in fact he was looking at her with such censure in every line of his expression, seen in the clear moonlight?

'Do you know anything about this sudden desire to leave Paxados?'

Stacey flinched. 'Why should I know anything about Chrysoula?' she countered.

'I thought her movements were of importance to you, since they seemed to concern Colin and you are very interested in that young man.'

She tried to turn her face away. What could she reply to his determined cross-examination? But he took her chin in one hand, still holding her firmly by the shoulders, his arm around her so that to an onlooker it would have looked almost as if he were embracing her. She was painfully aware of his steel-like strength and of the implacable expression of that mouth that she had seen curved to gentleness on some happier occasions.

'Tell me the truth, Stacey. That money that you borrowed was for Chrysoula, wasn't it?'

She nodded, unable to speak.

'I saw you blush when they said she had gone. You have a face that betrays you, my dear. That lovely translucent skin gives away your emotions too easily. Did you know that?'

Stacey was glad that at least it was not full day. If what he said was true, her face would be betraying her now. Her lips trembled and her eyes filled with tears, hard as she fought to hold them back.

'I hope this young man is worth your tears. You must be desperately in love with him to take the step of bribing Chrysoula to get her out of the way.'

Stacey gasped. So that was the conclusion he had drawn! He thought she had sent Chrysoula to Athens to leave a clear field for herself. How far from the truth this was. And yet what could she say? It was true she had provided Colin with the money. And she had asked Stavros for it, knowing it was intended for the other girl. Stavros shook her gently by the shoulders and his expression was almost tender – but perhaps that was a trick of the moonlight.

'You will say it has nothing to do with me, but I do not like to see a young girl humbling herself for a man of Colin's kind. If you marry him, what do you intend to do? You cannot bribe every woman who catches your husband's eye. And what about Alexandra? Would you like me to send her back to Athens so that her presence does not interfere with your plans? It would suit me very well too. But would she be willing to go?'

'You don't understand,' Stacey murmured. She felt helpless, too confused by his proximity and the powerful effect this had on her emotions to be able to reply logi-

163

cally to him.

'I think I understand very well. This quiet, shy exterior you show to the world at large hides a certain determination, but I am sorry, Stacey, that I feel your affections have been misplaced. You are young and inexperienced, but you are lovely, and that mouth, so soft and gentle, shows by its curves that you are made for passion. You should marry a man worthy of you, Stacey, not an irresponsible wastrel who does not know how to conduct his life, let alone yours.'

Stacey thought of Alexandra, so in love with Colin, that she had said if she did not get him she would do something desperate. Was Colin a wastrel? Stacey did not think so. He was a man who up to now had been irresponsible, yes, wandering from girl to girl, never able to find the one who really suited him and tempted by the fact that his own charm was considerable where women were concerned. But fundamentally she did not think he was altogether bad.

'I don't think he's a wastrel,' she said. 'Up to now, I admit, he hasn't made much of his life, but he hasn't had as many advantages as other people. I think he could make something of his life if he married the right girl. And I think once he settled down he could be faithful. He only needs to love sincerely for this to be possible.'

Stavros looked at her. His mouth seemed to have a scornful smile. 'There is no convincing you, Stacey, is there? But perhaps it is as well for you to start out on your life with Colin filled by so much trust and faith. I only hope disillusionment does not come too soon.'

He got up to go, and she was forced to follow. It seemed hopeless now to try to explain that her interest in Colin was purely that of an onlooker now. For if she tried to gain his favour for Colin on Alexandra's behalf it would only make matters worse.

He turned back to help her over a rough part of the path and as he did so she stumbled so that she fell against him. He grasped her arm rather roughly and she felt disturbed by his touch but too weary to shrug away from him.

'I hope you will not be offended if I ask you to do nothing indiscreet while you are under my roof. I realize you consider yourself engaged to Colin and in the opinion of English girls I understand this allows certain liberties, but I still feel responsible for your well-being, strange as this may appear to you.'

'Let's leave the subject alone now,' she murmured tiredly. 'I've said before that you don't understand the situation and that it's no use trying to explain. You can be sure I'll try to do nothing to disturb you while I'm here. And as soon as I've paid back the money you lent me I'm prepared to go.'

'Do not let the question of money worry you. You are at liberty to go at any time.'

Did this mean he wanted her to go immediately? She dared not ask, for in her heart she knew that she wanted to stay. Whatever this man thought of her, she wanted to be near him and could not bear the idea of deliberately placing miles of sea and land between herself and him.

The next day was Good Friday and Dimitraki came to visit Socrates and keep him company while the family went with their visitors to see the procession in the village, the ceremony of the Epitaphios, the funeral procession of the dead Christ. Dimitraki brought with him a small basket of hardboiled eggs dyed a bright red, and Sophia told Stacey that this was a Greek custom symbolizing the blood shed by the dying Christ.

Sophia was dressed in black with a dark wrap over her head and shoulders and Stavros was in a formal dark suit when they assembled to go down to the village. Lauren had made the facile excuse that she had a headache, saying to Stacey that this was 'not her scene', but she had assured Stavros that she would look after Socrates if he needed her and he had smiled his approval of this. Niko was in a dark suit and looked more serious than usual, but in spite of the solemnity of the occasion, Colin found something to say that brought responsive giggles from Alexandra and a frown to the older man's face.

Stacey wore a white dress and Sophia had lent her a black mantilla, but her honey-gold hair gleamed beyond the darkness of the lace and escaped in curling strands on each side of her face. Taking lanterns in their hands, they started the steep walk down the path. The village, when they arrived, was strangely silent. Usually at this time in the evening there was the sound of people released from their work and looking forward to an evening of conversation and music, the sound of clinking glasses and the smell of meat being grilled on spits and other savoury fragrances. But tonight there was a hush. No children cried. Even the dogs and goats were quiet and the cats which usually haunted the *tavernas* in pouncing hordes must have been shut away, for they were absent from the scene.

When they came to the open space in front of the church, the paved plaza was packed with people holding candles of dark brown wax. Their hands, sheltering the flames from the small night breeze, showed pink and translucent; decorations of ferns, flowers and palm fronds had been put up in front of the church and the crowd spoke only in murmurs, waiting for the procession to arrive.

Stacey found herself pressed up close between Sophia and Stavros. But soon Sophia turned and disengaged herself in order to talk to Niko. Alexandra and Colin had been divided by the press of the crowd from the others and were standing a little way off. Alexandra's olive skin glowed rosily in the candlelight and her large dark eyes gazed adoringly at Colin as he bent to speak to her. Stacey hoped that Stavros did not notice them. There was a sudden surge of the crowd as some activity manifested itself farther up the street and she found herself almost swept off her feet. Stavros put his arm around her. It was an instinctive desire to protect her, she knew, something that he would have done for any woman who was threatened with being crushed by the crowd, but her heart beat faster and she found it difficult to concentrate on the scene before her as the leaping flames of the candles swam and glittered before her eyes.

There was a sudden blaze of light from the floodlights that had been set up to illuminate the front of the church and at the same time in the distance there could be heard the sound of a drum, muffled and melancholy. Pressing its way through the throng, the band arrived first. Then came the children in their best clothes, carrying garlands of flowers as they walked solemnly before the bier which was borne shoulder-high, its great cloth embroidered with the figure of Christ in silver and gold. Behind came the boy scouts and naval cadets marching in order, then the Mayor and officials of the village, and the fishermen with their brown weather-beaten faces. The band played on, repeating the same heart-piercing lament that had the same effect, Stacey thought, as bagpipes heard from the walls of some old Scottish castle. It seemed to her, standing within the shelter of his arms, that Stavros and herself together with all the people in the village square were caught up in a terrible sadness from which there seemed no relief.

When at last they returned to the house, she went to her room quite soon and had already changed into a nightdress with its matching negligée when she heard Socrates calling to her. Dimitraki had gone home already and she had thought Sox would be asleep, but he was sitting up wide-eyed, his face a little flushed, his expression anxious.

'Stacey, I asked Dimitraki to look at Flavia for me, but he couldn't find her in the stable.'

'But you know she often wanders and she usually comes back quite safely.'

'But tonight I am afraid. Suppose someone finds her and takes her for their Easter feast?'

Stacey thought this very unlikely, because the people in the village had great respect for other people's property, but it was not altogether impossible. In any case she did not want Sox to worry about it, so she decided the only thing to satisfy him would be to go and find the little animal.

By now it was well after midnight, but it was still mild and she hardly thought she would meet anyone on the path to the citadel at this hour, so she did not change from her negligée and nightdress. She quickly found her way there, but although the moon had risen and the scene was quite clear, she could see no sign of the little creature, nor even hear the sound of his bleating. The night was still and hushed as if the shadow of the funeral procession they had just witnessed lay over the island. But suddenly she heard some kind of noise. It was too high a sound to be a goat. No, it sounded human, more like laughter. But it was below here. It must be near the bathing beach. Who could be there at this time? The night was warm, but tonight hardly seemed to be the time for indulging in a moonlit bathe.

Just then Stacey thought she heard the sound of Flavia's plaintive bleat farther down the path and hastened to investigate. Yes, there she was standing on a rock in the moonlight, her horns traced in silver, her fleece gleaming white. Stacey called softly, but she tossed her head and, with a flick of the tail and even, it seemed, a wicked glance from her dark eyes, she was off down the path in the direction of the bathing hut. The door was closed, but she butted it ajar and followed by Stacey rushed into the room. There was a gasp and a startled exclamation and, to Stacey's great confusion, she found she had interrupted Colin and Alexandra, who had obviously planned a meeting there.

Her embarrassment gave way to indignation. Colin had no right to compromise a young girl like Alexandra. Stavros would be furious if he knew. They had sprung up from the chaise-longue and were looking at her with mingled expressions of indignation and apprehension. Colin was the first to recover his poise.

'Stacey, thank God it's you! I thought for a moment it might be Sophia or worse still, Stavros.'

He was clad only in a pair of bathing trunks, and

Alexandra, who was in her orange bikini costume, took a towelling wrap and quickly put it on, shivering with nervous apprehension. Her large dark eyes gazed imploringly at Stacey.

'You two are very foolish to come here at this time. I thought you would have more sense, Colin. You know Stavros would be furious if he knew about it.'

Alexandra had recovered from her fright and now pouted a little.

'There's no need to be so prim, Stacey. That procession was so wearying we decided to slip away and have a midnight swim. What harm is there in that?'

'I don't know. It depends on you, of course. But I'm sure of this – that your family would disapprove of it if they knew. Why can't you have the sense to be careful? You'll never get their approval for your marriage if you behave like this.'

Colin held up his hand. 'Sh . . . I thought I heard something. Yes, there's someone else walking down the path.'

'It's Stavros,' said Alexandra, who had rushed to the window. 'What can we do now? Colin, he mustn't see me. It would ruin everything if he thought we had met at this hour by ourselves. His ideas are so strict. He should have lived a hundred years ago!'

Flavia, who had been remarkably quiet up to now, mainly because she was chewing a bathing cap she had found, now made a small scuffling noise and drew Colin's attention.

'Go out the back way and take Flavia with you,' he suggested to Alexandra. 'Stacey can stay with me. Stavros may not come in. He's probably just going for a walk, and if you run into him, you could say you were searching for the goat for Sox.'

Alexandra seized the little animal's lead.

'You don't mind, do you, Stacey? Even if Stavros sees you with Colin, it can hardly matter, because you aren't his family and quite soon you will be leaving.'

Everything had been decided so quickly that Stacey had little choice in the matter. Even if she had had time to think about it she would probably have consented to the plan of action, for she knew how furious Stavros would be about Alexandra arranging a meeting with Colin at this late hour and in this lonely place. The Greek notions of propriety in the womenfolk of the family were very strict. If Stavros knew of this meeting he would insist that Colin leave the island.

'I'll go out and try to head Stavros off,' Colin suggested, putting a wrap over his costume. 'Stacey, you'd better stay here for the time being.'

Stacey stood behind the half-open door and heard Colin go along the path. Alexandra, fleetfooted as the little goat she was leading, would find her way easily up to the house by a steeper way amongst the trees. She heard Colin greet Stavros. He was some yards away, but in the still night she could hear almost every word.

'Hello, Colin, what are you doing here at this hour? I thought I was the only one who was addicted to midnight walks. But I see you have been swimming.'

He sounded good-natured enough. Evidently he was not in the least suspicious of the true situation.

'Yes, I often have a midnight swim when I can't sleep,' she heard Colin say.

'It seems rather a cold pastime at this time of the year, but everyone to their own tastes. The sea doesn't warm up properly until June.'

She heard Colin laugh easily. 'You, having been brought up in this marvellous climate, have different standards from a poor Englishman! The water seems warm to me here even at Easter.'

'Well, I won't keep you. I'm just going down to the beach to check up that my dinghy has been pulled above high water mark. Our servants are apt to be a little forgetful when they are celebrating the Easter Festival.'

Footsteps passed quite near to the hut and a little while later Colin put his head round the door.

'All clear now. He's on his way down to the beach, but I don't think we'd better go back together, Stacey. I'll go first and try to catch up with Alexandra to tell her everything is all right. I'd be glad if you would wait a while, just to make sure. You could intercept him if he comes back too quickly and seems likely to catch up with us.'

There was nothing Stacey wanted less than to encounter Stavros at this time. She closed the door of the beach hut and settled herself down to wait. She dared not light the lamp, but the moonlight illumined the room with its own pale light. She realized only now how tired she was and thought that if she had to spend some time here she might as well be comfortable, so put her legs up on the chaise-longue and rested her head against the soft cushioned back, drawing the light woven coverlet over her bare legs. In a few minutes, struggle as she might to avoid it, she was sound asleep.

A slight sound woke her and she opened her eyes reluctantly, seeming to come from some place miles away and not at all sure where she could be at this moment. Then she realized that the sound she had heard was that of footsteps returning up the path. Thank goodness, that must be Stavros on his way back. Now all she had to do was to wait a while longer and she could go back to her own bed. But she must not fall asleep again. She sat up now, trying to sort out her ideas about the events of the night.

At any rate a catastrophe seemed to have been averted, for Alexandra had evidently got back safely and there had been no need for herself to take any blame for the meeting with Colin. And perhaps they would have learned their lesson and be more careful in future. Surely now she could go. It was a long time since she had heard the footsteps. She yawned sleepily. How glad she would be to get some sleep! The moon was lower now and as she set off up the path there were deep patches of shadow under the sea-wracked olive trees.

Thank goodness, now there was the end of the path with the broken columns shining silver beyond. But there, silhouetted against the pale columns, was a dark figure, a figure still as one of the classical statues that must have adorned these ruins when it was a living temple to the gods. She stood still and Stavros approached her until he was within touching distance. Then he paused and she could not turn aside, for he barred her path as he looked down at her from his superior position.

'There seems to be an amazing number of sleepless people wandering around Paxados during the hours of night,' he said. 'Were you another one suffering from insomnia, Stacey?'

'I went to look for Flavia,' she said. It was the first thing that came into her head.

'This little animal provides a good excuse for midnight jaunts. You seem rather indiscreetly dressed for goat-hunting.'

For the first time, Stacey became aware how she must look to him, with her hair dishevelled, and her body scantily clad in a short diaphanous gown.

'I should have changed. It was foolish of me, but I didn't think it would take long and I didn't realize I would meet anyone at this time.'

'No?' His smile mocked her. 'I think you did, Stacey. I met Colin coming out of the beach hut some while ago.'

'But you don't even know that I was with Colin,' Stacey said indignantly, for she felt hemmed in on all sides by circumstances beyond her control.

'I opened the door of the beach hut a short while ago. You were sleeping very peacefully. I must have disturbed you when I went away.'

'But I wasn't with . . .' Stacey stammered out, and then realized she could hardly deny that she had been with Colin without involving Alexandra and muddling the situation still further.

'You looked very sweet, very innocent in your sleep, Stacey. But your actions don't accord with your appearance, do they? However, what you do is your own business, I suppose.'

His tone was moderate and she was surprised when he suddenly seized one of the pieces of marble that lay loosely on a low wall of the citadel and smashed it on to the ground as if he were killing a snake. The sudden noise disturbed the multitude of swallows that were nesting in the broken leaves of the temple and for a while the air was filled with the small arrows of their bodies poised in startled flight. This unexpected violence from a man usually in complete control of himself, the noise of the crashing stone, the shrill twittering of the birds, all unnerved Stacey and she turned to him with flaring anger.

'Why did you do that? See how you've disturbed the swallows!'

He seized her roughly in his arms.

'You are a strange enigma to me, Stacey. So much concern for little things, so much emotion wasted on unworthy objects. Colin is playing with you as he played with Chrysoula. Oh, yes, I know now. Her father told me she got the money from Colin and I surmised that he had borrowed it from you. How can you lend yourself to such shamelessness? And knowing Colin and what he has done, how could you be so indiscreet in your own behaviour tonight?'

'My life is my own business. It has nothing to do with you.'

'Hasn't it? We will see about that.'

And now he was kissing her, fierce angry kisses that held passion but little tenderness. She could feel the implacable strength of him directed against her, hostile and strange as the rippling might of a tiger. With all her power she willed herself to stand rigid in his arms, and at last, sensing her total lack of response, he let her go.

'So. I cannot impress you? You do not think that a man's kisses are worth more than those of a weakling?'

Stacey was torn with bitter regret now. If only she could have felt herself able to respond to his kisses in absolute surrender, but he had only been punishing her. It was his way of showing that he thought her loose and immoral. One thing was clear to Stacey now. She could stay at Paxados no longer. After tomorrow she must go.

CHAPTER TWELVE

'WE can go after Easter, if you like,' Lauren announced next morning over their coffee and rolls. 'I'm becoming bored and I'd like to get back to London. I don't seem to be getting anywhere with either Stavros or Niko. Niko is just a philanderer out for anything he can get from a girl, and Stavros seems unresponsive and too devoted to that tiresome little boy. I don't seem able to make any impression on him at all, and now I don't know whether I even want to. No, I'm quite ready to go back to London. We'll arrange a flight as soon as you like. On Monday, if possible.'

Stacey was relieved, for this fitted in with her own plans. After last night she was determined to leave Paxados. She could not bear it any more to be near Stavros and know that the only feeling he had for her was one of contempt. He believed that she was having an affair with Colin, and whether they intended to marry eventually or not, the very fact that he thought she had been unchaste was against his strict Greek code of the behaviour expected of women.

Sophia went about her tasks for the Easter Festival seemingly unaware of the emotional upsets in the household. She asked Stacey to go down to the village for something she needed and Stacey was very glad to have the walk in the clear sunlit air. She had learned to love this little island with its friendly people and she hated the thought that after tomorrow she would never see it again. On the quayside there were more people than usual seated on chairs at the *kafenion* because the fishermen had not taken out their boats today. Amongst the white-painted buildings, small boys ran hither and thither with swinging trays bearing cups of black coffee and glasses of water to the customers. It was a sad day, thought Stacey, for lambs. In the streets people were carrying them firmly grasped under their arms and plaintive bleats filled the air, for it was the Easter custom that every household should have a lamb, flavoured with oreganum, roasted on a spit and basted with olive oil and lemon.

As she was walking back up the path, the sea spread itself in colours of green and turquoise edged by a ruffle of lacy white foam, and the land breeze blew from the heights with its scent of thyme and pine needles where curtains of spun-silk mists were whirling away from the citadel. When she was in the heart of the city she would remember this.

The kitchen, when she entered with her purchases, was a scene of bustling activity with Sophia directing operations in the calm soothing manner which seemed necessary in view of the servants' excitement. There was a beautiful smell of fresh yeasty baking and of savoury soup which would be eaten when they returned from church after midnight. And already a lamb was turning on the spit in the great open fireplace. It was a fascinating kitchen, Stacey thought, with very modern equipment but a feeling of a place that had been used for many years, with shining copper ware on the shelves and old blue plates on the dressers.

'Stacey, I am so glad that you are to be here for the most important Greek celebrations,' said Sophia, beaming. Stacey, who had become very fond of her, felt heart-sore when she realized she would have to part from her soon and never see her again. She felt it was a poor return for Sophia's kindness to announce abruptly that they were going, but what could she do? She decided she had better tell her straight away.

'Yes, Sophia, I'm glad too that I have been able to stay for Easter, but I'm afraid we will have to go soon.'

Sophia looked surprised.

'But, my dear, I thought you would be able to stay a while longer. Surely you don't mean you intend to go directly after Easter?'

'I'm afraid so. Lauren has decided she had better take up some offers of modelling in London.'

'Ah, Lauren, yes. But there is no need for you to go, my dear. Socrates has grown so fond of you. Indeed we all have. I had hoped you could be persuaded to stay until we go back to Athens at the end of summer. But perhaps it is boring for you and I am being selfish?'

Stacey turned her head away, finding it hard to keep back her tears when she was faced with the older woman's kindness.

'You mustn't think me ungrateful ... I would have loved to stay but ...'

Sophia looked at the brimming eyes and took her firmly by the arm.

'A little sherry is indicated. We have all been working too hard lately. Come into the pantry, where we can have a little peace.'

There were two rush-bottomed chairs in the large pantry and Sophia unlocked a cupboard from which she took a decanter and two glasses. It was a large room with bottles of preserves of the colour of jewels on the top shelves and sides of smoked ham hanging from hooks in the ceiling. There was a homely smell of herbs and newly baked bread.

'Now tell me,' asked Sophia, 'what is all this about? Has Stavros been unkind to you? You must not take him too seriously. His manner is strict, but when you know him better you will find that he is truly a good man. You find him a little sombre, perhaps, but it was not always so. He has a great capacity for happiness, but his life after he married was difficult. Poor Maria! One should not speak ill of the dead. She was young and beautiful and her head was turned by too much flattery. She lived for a brilliant social life, and Stavros is not like that. His tastes are simple in spite of his great wealth.'

'Oh, Sophia, it's so difficult to explain to you. You've been so kind to me, but various things have happened which have given Stavros a bad opinion of me. I think he would prefer that I should go. And I would prefer it too.'

'Are you sure?' Sophia's kindly face was troubled. She could not bear anyone to be unhappy in this household. It offended her ideas of hospitality and she was deeply shocked that Stacey of all people should feel the need to go so suddenly. 'I cannot believe that this will not sort itself out. My dear child, you can have done nothing unbecoming to you. One only has to look at your face to see goodness and purity shining there. I would as soon have doubts about my own daughter.'

Stacey had felt a need to confide in Sophia, but when she mentioned Alexandra she realized how difficult the whole position had become.

'Sophia, we have an English saying, "Least said,

soonest mended" and I think it applies in this case. It's best that I should go.'

'I must speak to Stavros.'

'Oh, no, please don't do that. It would only do harm, Sophia, it's best left alone.'

Stacey went to pack her belongings, for she had inquired about the ferry boats and found there would be one that they could catch on Monday to take them to Piraeus and then they could get a plane from Athens. She would not tell Socrates she was going – she would prefer to leave this to Sophia. She spent the rest of the day with the little boy. It was painful that he was making eager plans about what they would do when he was allowed to get up. She felt dreadful that she was agreeing with him while at the same time she knew she would not be here after Monday.

When Stacey said she did not intend to go into the village for the midnight celebrations but preferred to stay to look after Sox, Sophia shook her head.

'There is no need. I have instructed one of the servants to stay within call. Surely, Stacey, even if you are going soon you would like to take the opportunity to join in an important Greek festival.'

She looked a little hurt, and again Stacey felt guilty that she had puzzled Sophia by her behaviour, but whether Sox had a companion or not she intended to stay away from the celebrations. She could not bear to be near Stavros amongst the crowd at that emotion-packed ceremony when new hope comes to the world.

From her window she saw them go – Stavros, Niko, Lauren and Sophia. She heard Sophia calling for Alexandra, who responded from her room that she would follow soon. She was not quite ready yet, she said, and would see them near the church a little later. With mingled feelings, Stacey watched Stavros walking down the hill. How accustomed she had become to the dear sight of his dark head and the slim height of him. She had got over her feelings for Colin, so now she must get over her feelings for Stavros. But she knew that this emotion was very different from the immature sensations that had been the result of Colin's flattering attentions when she first came to London.

She sat on the balcony of her room, not lighting the lamp because she preferred to sit in the cool darkness thinking of Stavros. How long she had been sitting there she did not know, but she suddenly became aware of the clip-clop of donkeys' hooves and the sound of voices below.

'Thank goodness everyone seems to have gone into the village,' said Alexandra's voice. 'Oh, Colin, isn't this exciting? Won't it be marvellous to get away from all these rules and regulations and old-fashioned ideas?'

'Yes, it will. I'm tired of being treated like a ne'er-do-well. I want to show the world my lovely Alexandra, not have to steal around hiding the fact that I love her to distraction.'

'Oh, Colin, it's lovely to hear you say things like that. Are you sure you hired the boat for the right time?'

'Certain. He's to come to the quay at midnight when everyone is distracted by the Easter celebrations. And he's from another island, so he doesn't feel any loyalty to Stavros. All he's interested in is the money. By the way, you have remembered your jewellery?'

'Yes. The pearls and the ruby necklace that were left to me by my great-aunt I've never worn them, they are too old-fashioned, but I believe they are very valuable.

We should be able to sell them when we get to Athens.'

'Good. I have very little — you realize that? Only enough for immediate expenses and to pay the boatman.'

'Don't worry, darling. Once Mother and Stavros have got over the shock of our elopement they will have to accept the fact that we must marry and make some provision for us. After all, what else can they do?'

'Remember, the plan is that you should go to the market place first and appear quite natural. But before midnight when everyone is concentrating on the church ceremony, you must slip away and join me. I'll be at the quayside.'

'Oh, Colin, my dear love, not long to wait now!'

The voices died away and all Stacey could hear was the clip-clop of the donkeys' hooves trotting down the path. What could she do? She could not allow this to happen. She must follow them and try to prevent them from going. What madness it was! But typical of Colin. The night had turned cooler now and she put a cream-coloured cape with a hood over her thin dress, then she hastened down the path, hearing ahead of her the sound of the little donkeys but knowing she would not be able to catch up with them.

When she arrived at the Agora or market place, her heart sank, for all the people on the island had gathered there and it was very crowded. They held unlighted candles, this time made of white wax, and all eyes seemed to be turned towards the lighted doors of the little church. But there was Alexandra standing by herself. She had evidently not attempted to join Stavros and Sophia, who had been earlier arrivals. Of course they would think she had been held up by the crowd. But Stacey edged her way towards the young girl.

'Alexandra, I'm glad I've found you.'

'Stacey, what are you doing here? I thought you were not coming.'

Alexandra looked anything but happy to see her.

'I overheard you talking to Colin. Alexandra, forget it, please. What good will it do to go through with a crazy plan like that?'

'So you know. Well, I'm glad. Soon everyone else will know too. And it isn't a crazy plan, Stacey. It's the most sensible thing I've ever done.'

It was a good thing they were talking in English, for Alexandra's voice was getting louder and some of the crowd were turning interested but uncomprehending eyes towards them.

'But why are you doing it this way?'

'Because we are tired of concealment, tired of being patient. We love each other, and we can't wait for years and years waiting until Stavros with his stuffy old-fashioned ideas makes up his mind to notice we want to marry and decide whether Colin is suitable. Once I've gone away with him, they will have no alternative than to accept Colin. Good-bye, Stacey, you can't stop us now, so don't try.'

Before Stacey knew what was happening, Alexandra had slipped away through a gap in the crowd. Stacey thought the only thing to do now would be to go down to the quayside and try to talk some sense into Colin, so she wormed her way through the crowd in the direction of the harbour. It was a slow process and she got crushed and trodden on many times before she at last arrived there. And now she did not know where to look, for there were very many boats tied up and others anchored in deeper water and there was no movement to indicate where Colin was waiting and no sign of Alexandra.

She was standing gazing desperately over the dark water when she was startled by a deep voice behind her.

'What are you doing here, Stacey? I thought you had decided to stay at home.'

It was Stavros, darkly silhouetted against the scanty lights. Stacey considered the position swiftly. It was no use trying to conceal facts. The immediate need was to stop Alexandra from going with Colin. But how could she betray them to the one person who should not know? As she was about to speak, Stavros stepped forward until he was close by and could speak softly.

'One of the fishermen, who occasionally helps me with the yacht, heard another who had had a little too much ouzo telling his friend that Colin had hired a boat and intended to go to Athens with Alexandra. He came to find me in the crowd. Do you know anything of this?'

'I overheard them discussing it and I tried to argue with Alexandra, but she gave me the slip and came down here. It's so dark and I don't know where to look for them.'

'So you were trying to stop it too. I might have known.'

Stacey had no time to think what he meant by this, for at that moment Sophia appeared.

'Stavros, I came too. I could not bear to wait as you told me to. Where is Alexandra?'

'Don't worry, Sophia. We will find her.'

As he spoke they heard the put-put sound of a small boat heading out of the harbour and they could see a small red light swaying.

'It must be them,' said Sophia. 'Oh, heavens, how can they expect to reach Athens in that small boat? They are mad to think of it!'

'Aleko told me where his boat is moored. Stacey, will you come and help me sail it? Sophia, you must stay here. It's only a small boat and it would be better if you remained.'

'Very well, but oh, Stavros, please bring her back. I should have realized . . . I should have known of the danger and warned her . . . my little girl!'

The engine of the borrowed boat started without trouble and Stacey found herself once again skimming over the Aegean sea with Stavros. But how different this was from the previous journeys! It was dark and the sea was choppy inshore. They kept bumping over great waves and sliding down with a sickening jolt on the other side. But the boat in front of them seemed to be having a far worse time, for it rocketed from side to side as if it was not being properly guided. Gradually they gained on it and as they got away from the offshore waves the sea became calmer, but still the other boat continued to zig-zag in an alarming fashion and then, just as they were within yards of it, the nose thrust itself up into the air and the boat overturned

Stavros throttled down the engine and turned to Stacey.

'Hold her steady. I'm going over.'

'No, Stavros, no!'

'Don't worry. I will take a lifebuoy and the lifeline is attached. Keep the boat still We must try to keep them clear of the propellers.'

Stacey wished desperately that they had brought Niko or someone who could have helped Stavros in this predicament. She tried to guide the boat while she scanned the dark water and watched the lifeline tautening. There was a sudden call, reed-like and thin, from out of the gloom. Thank God, then, Alexandra was still alive, but how could Stavros find her? Stacey fumbled round in the boat and her hands touched a large torch, the kind that fishermen carry to shine on the water at night to see their catch.

The beam illumined the ink-blue, tossing waves and the small upturned boat to which two figures clung desperately. She felt the line tighten and saw Stavros swim with strong strokes towards the vessel. Guiding the boat, she managed to edge slowly nearer.

Alexandra was white, dripping and exhausted when Stavros at last managed to hand her over the gunwale. She lay weakly in the bottom of the boat like a half-drowned kitten as Stavros with Colin's help managed to right the other boat and take it in tow.

'But what about the other man?' asked Stacey. 'The owner of the boat?'

Alexandra raised her head.

'He didn't come. He was drunk, so we decided to take the boat ourselves. That's why it was so difficult to manage it. Colin said he could do it, but it was too rough.'

'But how did you think you could possibly get to Athens in that?' Stavros asked Colin sharply.

'We had arranged with the owner that we would leave it at his island and catch the ferry from there.'

Sophia was waiting on the quay, desperately anxious.

She enfolded Alexandra in her arms and ignored Colin who, mumbling something about going to the cottage to change, started to walk away.

'We will have a talk tomorrow,' Stavros said to him, 'when we have all recovered. Sophia, take Alexandra quickly back to the house. I will follow with Stacey when I have arranged about the boats.'

Stacey waited while he went along the waterfront and presently returned with Aleko, whom he left in charge. He had managed to borrow a fisherman's garb and, in his dark jersey and slacks, looked as Stacey had first seen him, so long ago, it seemed, on Delos.

She had expected him to be serious, but miraculously, or so it appeared to Stacey, he looked happier than she had ever seen him. He smiled at Stacey, the expression on his face brilliant and yet tranquil.

'If we hurry,' he said, 'you can still see the Easter Eve ceremony if you wish. It is five minutes to midnight.'

The crowd in front of the church was even denser. As they held the unlighted tapers, people kept asking each other the time and arguing about the correctness of their watches. Stavros put his arm around Stacey and held her warmly clasped in his arms. Was this just for protection against the crowd or did the dark glowing eyes and the smiling lips convey a deeper message?

'Forgive me, Stacey. I realize I have been wrong about you. Alexandra told me when she was in the water that it was she who had been in the beach hut with Colin, not you. Poor child, she thought she was drowning and must confess her sins.

'But I am sorry,' he added, 'if these events have disappointed your hopes. I know you had hoped to marry Colin yourself.'

Stacey shook her head. Whatever he thought of her she did not want to relinquish one moment of this blissful sensation of being in his arms.

'It was all a mistake,' she told him. 'I found when I arrived at the island that I didn't love Colin. I've never loved him. In London I was flattered by his attentions and mistook my feelings for real love. But here on Paxados I realized I was wrong.'

'And what made you realize you did not love him? Stacey, tell me, could it have been because that night when I first kissed you, you realized that you felt the same as I did?'

'As you did?' She could not believe his words could be sincere. But they must be. He would never lie to her.

'I thought . . . I was afraid it was all too obvious that I loved you. I tried to fight against it when I thought you loved Colin, but it was no use.'

'But I . . . since I came to Paxados, since I met you, I've had no thoughts for anyone else. That's why at last I thought I must leave, because I couldn't bear to stay here knowing you despised me.'

'Despise you? How can you say such a thing? I love you, Stacey, love you with all my heart.'

There was a sudden clash of sound, the bells pealing for midnight, and the crowd surged forward. From the great doors of the church came choirboys carrying tapers to light the white candles. The light from the altar spread amongst the crowd until the square blazed with small steadfast flames. *'Christos Aneste.'* 'Christ is risen.' All around them people were greeting each other, giving kisses on both cheeks. And there were shouts of joy as rockets shot upwards into the deep-blue sky showering streamers of stars.

But Stacey, safe in Stavros' sheltering arms, felt alone in a secret world, a magic place that was waiting to be explored, as she lifted her face to receive the kiss that was not for Easter alone but for a lifetime.

Why the smile?

... because she has just received her **Free Harlequin Romance Catalogue!**

... and now she has a complete listing of the many, many Harlequin Romances still available.

... and now she can pick out titles by her favorite authors or fill in missing numbers for her library.

You too may have a **Free Harlequin Romance Catalogue** (and a smile!), simply by mailing in the coupon below.

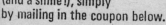

Golden Harlequin Library

A Treasury of Harlequin Romances!

Many of the all time favorite Harlequin Romance Novels have not been available, until now, since the original printing. But on this special introductory offer, they are yours in an exquisitely bound, rich gold hardcover with royal blue imprint. Three complete unabridged novels in each volume. And the cost is so very low you'll be amazed!

This very special collection of classic Harlequin Romances would be a distinctive addition to your library. And imagine what a delightful gift they'd make for any Harlequin reader!

Start your collection now. See reverse of this page for **SPECIAL INTRODUCTORY OFFER!**

v